HITCHED

PIPPA GRANT

LILI VALENTE

Michaela,
May your alpacas
never be lonely.
Pippa Grant ♥

ABOUT THE BOOK

Hitched

She's the last woman on earth I'd marry....again.
Yet here I am.
Saying my vows. Again.
To save an alpaca.
At least, that's my story.
But the truth might be a little more complicated.
I didn't want to let her go the first time. But now I have a second chance to win over my wife.
We're older. Wiser. And hornier.
This time, I won't fail.

Hitched is a red hot, enemies-to-lovers laugh-a-palooza featuring a girl in need of a marriage of convenience and a man in need of a cold shower to keep from falling for his fake wife. They say opposites attract, but with Blake and Hope, they also combust...

ONE

Blake O'Dell
(aka a man unaware he's about to repeat his biggest mistake)

There comes a time in every man's life when he needs to mind his own business.

For me, that moment is right now.

Yep.

This is me.

Minding my own business.

Turning around in the morning sunshine, walking away from the Happy Cat courthouse where the magnolias are blooming and the spring pollen is turning parked cars a sickly yellow-green and Hope St. Claire is sitting on the wide steps of the red brick building in a wedding gown, her light brown hair brushing the tops of her shoulders and a wilted bouquet of dandelions clutched in one hand.

I have places to be. Errands to run. Jobs to do.

So she's apparently getting married, and I had no idea

she was even dating anyone seriously. So I didn't recognize her at first, because that puffy meringue dress is so far from what she normally wears. So what?

It's none of my damn business.

And I sure as hell don't want to watch her marry someone else.

And yet, she called me. Said she had a job for me, and to meet her at the courthouse...

I've been doing odd jobs around town while I wait for my grape vines to mature. And seeing as she short-circuits electronics just by looking at them, I've done a lot of work for Hope St. Claire.

Unfortunately.

But whatever she needs in a wedding gown on the courthouse steps isn't a job I'm up for. Especially when my time is better spent pestering Gary at the Department of Revenue office about the liquor permit application he's sitting on for my tasting room, so I can quit doing odd jobs around town and get my winery off the ground.

With her head drooped the way it is, Hope hasn't spotted me yet, so I ease back into my pickup truck and start the engine nice and quiet.

As quietly as I can, anyway. I'm about to pull away from the curb when Hope drags a hand through her hair, granting me a glimpse of her miserable-looking face.

Guilt grips my nuts and holds them for ransom, because for all the irritation Hope brings to my life, she's still a person.

And a neighbor.

Neighbors are important in Happy Cat. Love or loathe each other, everyone here seems to understand that the only way we're getting through the hard times is together.

And hard times come around for all of us. Not a single person is immune.

I shift in my seat to try to take the pressure off my balls. The bobblehead hula man that my brothers glued to my dash as a joke wiggles his hips and strums his ukulele, silently encouraging me to lighten up and do the right thing.

I told her I was on my way, after all.

"I know, I know," I grumble. "But I didn't know she'd be dressed like—like—*that*."

I really don't care for the sight of Hope in a wedding dress.

It's bringing back reflux-flavored memories.

You know the kind, the ones that sit in your gut and throw poison darts at your lungs and heart, making you feel like you're going to lose your lunch.

That's pretty much how I feel every time I look at Hope. She does things to me. Bad things. Confusing things. Poison-dart-in-the-heart kinds of things...

"Chin up, kid, you're going to be fine," I whisper. To her, but maybe to myself too. "You always are. But I've got to sit this one out."

There's no way she could have heard me. I'm half a block away, inside my truck with the windows closed. But still, her head lifts, our eyes meet, electricity crackles through the air, and the need to make tracks grows so intense that my hand reaches for the gearshift without my conscious permission.

But I don't drag the handle down.

I'm not a runner or a responsibility dodger. I'm a good person who works hard and keeps my word.

It's usually so easy. But not with Hope. Nothing's easy with her, and it hasn't been for a damned long time.

Gut twisting, I kill my engine, and climb out, pretending I just got there.

"Knock out power to the entire block?" I call as I approach across the cracked sidewalk. "Or just the building?"

She starts to lift her hand—undoubtedly to flip me the bird—but then drops it into her lap over the lacy wedding dress with a sigh.

"Give me two minutes and an open mind," she says wearily. "I have a strange proposition for you."

"Stranger than usual?"

"Way stranger. But you're going to seriously consider it, because that's the plan."

I grunt. "Sounds like a terrible plan."

She waves her saggy bouquet at me. "Seriously. Don't start with me today. My grandmother died and—"

"I'm sorry," I say, meaning it. I didn't know her gram, but I know several of Hope's animals came from her, so I assume she was a good woman. But I'm still not sure what that has to do with me. Or this dress. "You do know that most people go with black for mourning, right?"

Her cheek twitches, and if she glares at me any harder, she'll probably sprain her eyeball.

Can't say I blame her. That was a dick thing to say.

But she brings out the worst in me.

"You know my sanctuary was designated as the official guardian of Gram's pets and livestock when she went into nursing care last year, right?" she asks.

"I've heard about it a time or two." More like seven times a day, with how often she needs handyman assistance and how many of those animals need special care.

"Now that she's gone, I've learned that her will dictates that the entirety of her estate—her farm, her house, everything, including her animals—goes to whichever of her grandchildren gets married first. That means my cousin Kyle could get custody of my animals if I don't get married *fast*."

This is where I should have a snappy comeback, because I know for a fact that Hope got married first.

But we don't talk about that.

Ever.

I try to concentrate on the part where she wants to take care of her grandmother's animals, but all I can see are neon lights, Elvis, and cameras flashing inside the Little Chicken All You Can Eat Snack Chapel.

Then annulment papers less than 24 hours later.

Yeah. There's a solid reason Hope and I don't get along, and it has nothing to do with how I feel about her, and everything to do with her not feeling the same way about me.

So chatting about her getting married? This is worse than having my nuts stuck in a vise. I'd rather be in a cage with a hundred feral monkeys who want to use my cock as a rope swing than talk about Hope getting married.

She taps her dandelion bouquet against her dress. "I went to a website—no, don't say it, because *yes*, I can occasionally use electronics without them exploding, if I hold my breath and try really hard—and I found a guy who was willing to marry me for a few grand—"

I make a noise—this story is getting worse with every passing second—but she shushes me by shaking the bouquet again, sending a wilted yellow flower flying my way.

"But," she continues, "he brought his father with him to be the witness, and it turns out his dad has a pacemaker. So when we met and shook hands..."

Oh, shit.

My brother Jace's wife, Olivia, who is deep into crystals and auras and spiritual woo-woo, keeps telling us that Hope is something called a *wiper*, which supposedly means she has extra-magnetic blood that gives off computer- and electronics-killing vibes.

I've never bought into hocus-pocus, but I've also never met anyone who could short-circuit a microwave from halfway across the room when it wasn't running either.

"Did you kill the guy?" I ask, my throat tight.

"Can you just listen for *two minutes* without interrupting?"

"Hope. Jesus. That's not a *no*."

"The EMTs think he's going to be fine," she grumbles. "But now Frederick doesn't want to get married, because he's scared of me, even though I promised I'd never touch his father again upon penalty of being eaten alive by wild hogs. But I need to get married *now*, Blake, before Kyle gets smart enough to think of the same plan."

And I need to quit staring and pick my jaw up off the floor.

But the one thing Hope St. Claire has never failed to do is leave me speechless.

"So, basically, I'm out of options," she finishes. "Which is why I called you. I'm throwing myself at your mercy, but I promise to make it worth your while. I know you're fighting the county for a liquor license for your tasting room, and I *do* have a *very* good relationship with the Department of Revenue staff. After everything I had to go through to get the farm licensed as a shelter, Gary and I are tight. And I'm willing to use my connection for your benefit."

"Whoa, wait a minute—"

"We don't have to stay married forever," she rushes on. "Just for long enough for me to get legal possession of the animals and ensure they'll live long, healthy, happy lives. And then we can tell everyone we made a big mistake and move on. Easy peasy."

"Like you did last time?" I ask, hating the hint of pain in my voice. It's been four years. It shouldn't still sting, but it does.

Her brown eyes snap to mine again, and her cheeks flush pink. "I have no idea what you're talking about."

Right.

Because last time *didn't happen*. That's what we agreed on.

But it did happen, and it left scars behind, and I can't fathom how Hope convinced herself asking *me*, of all fucking people, to marry her was a good idea.

Dammit. Now I'm getting hot in the face.

"I just want to make sure all the animals have a good forever home," she says, pressing her hands together as a pleading furrow forms between her brows. "You know the only thing Kyle cares about is money. He'd stud out Chewpaca twenty-four seven to make gourmet alpaca babies, while the rest of the livestock and the dogs and the peacock and the ferret end up eating each other to survive and Chewpaca eventually gets so exhausted his penis falls off."

I snort, but I'm not in the headspace to laugh, even if the thought of poor Chewpaca banging his dong off is kind of funny.

I'm still stuck on the *we should get married* part.

The first time she proposed to me, she was holding hands with Jack Daniels and Captain Morgan as she cooed, *You're the best guy, Blake. The nicest and funniest and the best. I bet you'd kick ass at marriage. And you have the prettiest elbows. Is it weird that I love your elbows? 'Cause I really do...*

I wasn't so sober myself—clearly, if *you have the prettiest elbows* was all it took to convince me to cruise down the aisle.

Today, however, I'm so sober I'm in danger of dehydration. I'm also older and wiser and not about to open myself up to this particular kind of pain again. "I'm sorry, Hope, I get that you're in a hard spot, but—"

"This is *not* my first choice, believe me," she cuts in. "But if it's between blackmailing you into marrying me, or watching Kyle take off with Chewpaca and other innocent animals he'll abuse, I'm sorry, but the fur babies win. Lives are hanging in the balance, Blake, so I'm getting married. *Now*."

She's serious.

But there's no fucking way I'm marrying her today. Or tomorrow. Or ever again. "You don't have any blackmail material on me, Hope, and I'm out of here."

"Wait!" She springs to her feet, scattering flower petals from her fluffy white princess skirt. "Okay, forget the blackmail part. Think of it as a job! You do odd jobs, and you're never going to get a job odder than this one."

"I can't marry you."

She heaves a sigh. "If this is about that thing that we don't talk about—ever—then let me assure you, it didn't happen. But if it had happened, it would have proven that you can, in fact, marry me anytime you want."

"Marriage should be about love and commitment." Which it *was*.

For me, at least.

For her...

"I'd argue that marriage is a business contract, but I can also promise that this *is* about love," she insists. "It's about the universal love of animals and doing what's right. You've met Chewpaca. Can you imagine his life being turned into one long string of bad hook-ups? He's the world's top alpaca stud. An ounce of his sperm is worth more than your entire vineyard. Do you know what Kyle would do with that kind of money tree? Chewpaca could be seriously hurt."

I do know the alpaca. Apparently his fur—wool?—is top-notch.

Sweet animal. Loves my sister-in-law.

But the poor guy is going to have to find himself another savior, and Hope another sucker. "Sorry, you need to ask someone else."

"Who?"

Well, shit. "Tucker," I say, then cringe, because Tucker's in a long-term relationship, and his girlfriend probably wouldn't appreciate that. Hope clearly doesn't either, because she gives me the hairy, *what the hell is wrong with you?* eyeball.

"Okay, okay," I mutter, "let me think." But the next three names that pop up on my mental screen are all too odd or have chronic body odor issues.

The four after that are old enough to be her grandfather. But maybe...

"Don't say it," she orders as my brows lift in contemplation.

"Say what?"

"You were going to suggest Carl or Frank."

"Well, if it's purely a fake marriage..."

"I agree, but *they already turned me down*. I'm not kidding, Blake. I'm out of options. You're it. My last chance."

"You asked Carl *and* Frank?" I ask dubiously, ignoring the voice in my head that's a little hurt to be lower on the list than those two cranky old coots.

"I. Love. That. Alpaca," she says. "And the other animals too."

"You asked *Carl*."

She brings her bouquet to her chest, squishing it between her fingers as she threads them together in a pleading gesture that tugs at my conscience. "You give me three months of marriage, long enough to ensure I'm named Chewpaca's legal owner and Kyle can't touch any of Gram's sweet babies. In exchange, you get your liquor license. And while we're married, you can be a workaholic at your vineyard, and I'll be a workaholic on the farm. We'll barely have to see each other. It'll be like the 'I do's' never even happened."

"Except when you fry a toaster or a milking machine."

"Does that mean you're on board?" she asks, hope lighting her eyes, making her look even prettier than she usually does. Which is too pretty.

I can't marry her. Not for all the liquor licenses in Georgia.

I shake my head, lifting my hands into the air at my sides. "No, it doesn't. I can't, Hope. I'm sorry."

I start to back away, but she stops me with a threat. "If you don't help me, I'm calling Olivia. She *loves* Chewpaca. What, exactly, do you think she'd do if she found out *you* were the reason he has to go to a horrible new home? If it's *your* fault that her baby daughter will never get the chance to know the alpaca who saved her mother's life?"

I'd accuse her of being melodramatic, except I know both Hope's cousin, the asshole who stands to inherit Chewpaca, and my sister-in-law. Olivia believes she has a cosmic connection with that damn alpaca, and Hope's not exaggerating any of this.

Plus, I *need* that liquor license. I've been denied three

times already for stupid red tape reasons, and my latest application will expire if I can't get the DOR to sign off soon.

But Gary has been dragging his feet again. I'm starting to think this is a personal vendetta for him, not simply a result of being dedicated to crossing every t and dotting every i. I suspect I'm being denied my license because Gary's pissed that my oldest brother, Ryan, helped put Gary's brother in jail last year.

Small-town life, small-town politics, small-town bullshit.

And sometimes the only way out of the poo pile is to convince someone with influence to put in a good word for you.

"*Please*, Blake?" Hope begs, and I feel myself starting to actually consider this insanity.

Death by penis yanking does seem like a cruel thing to do to Chewpaca.

And I need my liquor license.

And Hope—just *Hope*. Shit.

How can I hate her and want to be her hero at the same time?

"If I agree to this," my mouth says before my brain can object, "you have to say five nice things about me every day."

She blinks. "What?"

"I don't like being grumpy or angry, but you make me both, so you're going to have to say five nice things about me every day. Help me keep my sense of humor intact until the madness is over."

She presses two fingers to her visibly twitching left eyelid. "Fine."

"Wait. What about Gordon?" I say, inspiration striking

at the eleventh hour, right as the guillotine is about to fall. "Didn't he break up with his internet girlfriend last week?"

"He *also* turned me down." She sighs. "And I think they're already back together. Gordon doesn't like to leave his house or put on pants after he gets home from work. An online girlfriend is the best kind of girlfriend for that particular lifestyle."

Shit.

She asked the resident firebug taxidermist before she asked me too.

Now I'm getting pissed, because I'm *not* that low in the pecking order in this town.

Am I?

Do I need to work out more? Put on something other than work clothes once in a while? Learn something about hair products and how to apply them?

Or is it because she truly hates me that much?

My blood burns hotter at the thought, and I suddenly realize that I'm going to do this.

I'm going to marry the shit out of her.

Just to torture her with my presence.

Every single day.

"And you have to come to poker night with my family," I inform her.

"Good. I like your family."

Just not you.

That was the problem last time.

And it looks like that's going to be the problem all over again. But this time, I won't walk away with a broken heart. This time, it's all business, with a side of vengeful pleasure.

Maybe it's wrong to look forward to torturing my ex-wife with our second ill-advised marriage.

But if it's wrong, I don't want to be right.

TWO

Hope St. Claire
(aka a desperate woman with too many animals and not
enough options)

As I walk down the short aisle of the windowless green-carpeted courtroom where I'm marrying Blake O'Dell in approximately thirty seconds, I picture my grandma's alpaca.

Probably not what most brides picture on their wedding day, but Chewpaca is why I'm getting married.

I don't want my grandmother's land. I don't want her house.

I just want to give her animals a good life, because animals are the best part of my family. They're innocent and simple and they don't have passive-aggressive psychological battles over who hired the wrong maid or use their kids as go-betweens when they have a fight and aren't speaking to each other.

Nor do they write wills demanding that their heirs be *married*.

But hey, if I'm getting married, at least I'm doing it the St. Claire way.

To a man who's glowering at me like I'm his adversary on the field of battle as I join him in front of Judge Maplethorpe.

With those bright green eyes, thick, unruly hair, and big, strong, perfectly rough hands, Blake's exactly my type. Right down to the fact that he's dressed for working in the field instead of for a wedding.

Except that he wants forever, and I don't believe in it.

Not with the marriages I've seen up close and personal.

Oh, and he hates me, mustn't forget that tiny detail.

I feel guilty about bringing him into my chaos, but I was out of options.

Chewpaca can't go to Kyle.

Period.

"You have a lovely bride," Judge Maplethorpe murmurs to Blake as I come to a stop beside him in front of the bench.

Blake grunts dubiously, but covers with a clearly forced smile. "Brides are always beautiful when a man's in love."

I snort.

The judge frowns at me. He's in his sixties, with more hair coming out of his ears and nose than sitting on top of his head. His oldest daughter used to babysit me when my parents had to go to Atlanta for gala fundraisers and black-tie dinners.

She'd always sneak in the ingredients to make chocolate chip cookies, which my mom never kept on hand because *empty calories are the devil's handmaiden, Hope*. Judge Maplethorpe is not the kind of man who would understand a marriage of convenience between two old enemies.

We're going to have to sell this. At least a little.

I grab Blake's arm, which is just as sinfully sexy as his hands—I am *such* a sucker for a man who works outside and isn't afraid to get dirty—and say with a cheerfulness born of desperation, "Hitch us up, Judge."

"We have a honeymoon to get to," Blake agrees dryly.

The judge's eyes light up. "And where are you taking this lovely lady on your honeymoon?"

Blake winks at him. "That's a secret, but it'll be a trip neither of us will ever forget."

And now my belly's flipping and things low in my body are unzipping and I make a mental note to cuff myself to my four-poster bed before I go to sleep every night of my impending marriage.

In addition to blowing up electronics, I've also been known to sleepwalk, and the last thing I need to do is let my subconscious take control while I'm married to Blake. It might assume it's okay to indulge the hunger he awakens inside me, and that would be bad news for everyone.

But mostly me, since Blake would probably laugh me right off his front porch.

Ignoring my inappropriate case of tingles, I subtly dig my elbow into his side. "Oh, you," I say lightly.

Through gritted teeth.

Let's move this along already. Time's a-wastin'. Right now, Kyle thinks he has the upper hand because he met a girl on Tinder last week.

But he underestimated me.

I'm just glad I didn't have to resort to full-fledged groveling.

Or crying. I hate fake crying, though I'm pretty good at it after a childhood spent doing whatever it took to escape the magnifying glass of my parents' disapproval. But these wouldn't have been fake tears. Before Blake pulled up, I was on the verge of weeping on the courthouse steps.

He's saved the day, and I'm thankful for that, no matter how miserable I'm sure he's going to make me until Gram's will is legally executed and the animals are officially mine.

"All right, let's get you two hitched." The judge beams at me. "I used to worry about you, sweetheart, but you're getting one of the good ones here."

"Tell that to my parents," I joke through a smile, already dreading the "I eloped with a guy who isn't nearly as rich as you'd like for him to be" conversation I'm going to have to have with dear old Mom and Dad.

It's almost a relief that they've taken their chilly relationship to Europe for a summer getaway.

Otherwise, they'd probably be here objecting to everything from Blake's heritage to his work boots.

"Your parents love me, boo-boo-cakes," Blake grits out through his own smile.

Doubtful—also, boo-boo-cakes?—but I beam at him.

My cheeks hurt.

My skin itches, because dresses and I don't get along, but my mother would've double-killed me if I didn't wear one to my wedding.

The one that she'll know about, anyway.

My heart is achy and empty, like it's hit that point in a good romance novel where all is lost, only the author died before she could finish the story. And now the two characters she left behind will live in limbo, in the land where happily ever after never comes.

Kind of like Blake and me.

"So good to see you so happy," Judge Maplethorpe says again. He sighs, wipes a tear, opens a little black book, and starts the trial.

I mean wedding.

I cut a glance at Blake while the judge says his short bit about the sanctity of marriage. There's a muscle ticking in his jaw, and his green eyes are as hard as the petrified horse poop I tripped over in the pasture last week.

He's going to bolt.

Any minute now, he's going to realize that I'm a walking disaster, he wants no part of this, and he'll sprint for the door.

And I won't blame him.

I *am* a walking disaster. And he already knows—intimately—that I'm allergic to commitment. The only place I like romance is bound inside a book with a cover where the good guys always win and it's safe for anyone to fall in love, because it's not real.

But that hasn't stopped him from kissing me a time or two since that incident in Vegas that we don't talk about.

I shiver, and not just because this dress is showing off my milky white shoulders over the deep tan from midbiceps down. Actually, it's pretty freaking warm in this room.

Is the air conditioning broken?

I fan myself with my flowers, weeds picked fresh from the pasture this morning to symbolize that even weeds have a moment of beauty before they wilt and die and go spread their weediness everywhere else.

Like marriage.

It wilts.

It might not die—my parents are still together, even though they hate each other, and Kyle's parents too, since St. Claires aren't quitters—but it can get shriveled and sad as hell.

"Do you, Blake O'Dell, take this woman to be your lawfully wedded wife?"

So freaking hot in here.

"I do," Blake grits, then adds under his breath, "*again.*"

"Wonderful. And do you, Hope St. Claire, take this man to be your lawfully wedded husband?"

"If I have to."

The judge chuckles. "You always were the funny one."

I was never funny, and this courtroom is the temperature of Hell's sauna in August.

"And now the vows," Judge Maplethorpe says.

"I've written my own," Blake announces.

"*When?*" I ask, then belatedly remember to smile through the panic, because if he's written his, does that mean I have to write mine? "I mean, oh, pookie-pookie-poo, you shouldn't have."

"So sweet to see you so in love." Judge Maplethorpe wipes his eyes again. "Your families should be here for this."

"I'm getting it all on video," Griselda, the county clerk receptionist, announces. She's serving as witness, and the temperature in the room ratchets up another four degrees as I realize she's undoubtedly planning to post this to the town's InstaChat page as soon as we've sealed the deal.

"Your vows, Blake?" the judge prompts.

Blake turns to me with those angry dragon eyes and fire coming out his nostrils, and I'm suddenly less worried that he's going to bolt and more terrified that he's going to expose my plan to all of Happy Cat.

"Hope," he begins, and I stifle a squeak, because I've made my bed in asking him to marry me and now I have to take whatever comes.

And also be ready to tackle Griselda and make her delete the video.

"When I woke up this morning, I had no idea that in a few short hours my life would change forever," Blake continues. "I vow to you, here and today, to be the kind of husband you deserve, to always give as much as I get, and to never, ever forget how I feel in this moment."

Judge Maplethorpe blows his nose and takes a steadying breath. "Beautiful, Blake. Beautiful. Hope?"

The lights overhead start to buzz, and I realize I'm in trouble.

Olivia mentioned that stress can make my natural energy field go wonky, and I'm absolutely on the high end of the stress scale today. So I open my mouth and blurt the first thing that comes to mind.

"Blake, thank you for marrying me. I promise to try to make you as happy as you make me, so long as our marriage shall live."

The lights flicker, and I turn to the judge. "Could you get to the *now pronounce you* part before—"

There's a snap and a flash, and the room descends into total darkness.

"—that," I finish on a sigh.

"Oh well, we don't need electricity to have love and marriage," the judge's voice says somewhere in the darkness. "You want to add anything to your vows? Either one of you?"

"My phone died," Griselda says. "I can't get the screen to turn on so I can power up the flashlight feature."

"Of course not," Blake mutters.

"By the power vested in me by the state of Georgia, I now pronounce you man and wife," the judge's disembodied voice says. "You may now kiss the bride. Erm, if you can find her."

I make a kissing noise. "Good job, Blake! You found me. Now how about we—"

Before I can finish saying *get out of here so you can replace the fuses I just blew*, two strong hands grip my bare shoulders, two firm lips press to mine, and I suddenly remember *exactly* why I proposed to Blake four years ago in Vegas.

He kissed me on a dare from a blackjack dealer not long after we unexpectedly ran into each other that weekend. After one taste, I was drunker on him than I'd ever been on alcohol.

I'd never been kissed by a man who knew what he was doing before.

And this kiss?

Today?

In the blacked-out basement courtroom?

He's upping his game.

Using those firm lips to remind me of all the things he did to me in our hotel room on our first wedding night. His thumbs brushing my shoulders while his rough hands slide down my arms, teasing my skin until my whole body aches.

Pulling me tight against him, making my breasts heavy inside this stuffy dress, making me want his hands on my bare skin while his earthy scent floods my senses, taking me back to a fluffy hotel bed where he taught me that a talented man's tongue is better than a bucketful of sex toys.

Reminding me why I thought marrying him—the first time—was a good idea.

He's kissing all my memories out of the vault I've stored them in since we left Vegas.

There's a flickering and a buzz, and I realize it's not coming from my whacked-out energy field.

No, the lights are back on.

Someone must've flipped the circuit.

"So, so beautiful," Judge Maplethorpe chokes out.

Blake pulls out of the kiss and smirks down at me.

Anyone else would think it's a smile, but when it's aimed at me, it's a smirk.

And a promise—*There's more where that came from, Hope, and you know it.*

I do.

I very much do.

Which makes his promise a threat.

I'm doing this for Chewpaca, I remind myself.

And I'm not going to fall for my husband.

Because love always ends badly.

In my family anyway. St. Claires aren't built for forever.

And so Blake and I will just have to be business partners.

Without benefits.

"No benefits, no benefits, no benefits," I chant beneath my breath as I trail Blake out of the courtroom, already knowing that of all the promises I've made to myself in my life, this one is going to be the hardest one to keep.

THREE

From the text messages of Blake and Clint O'Dell

Blake: Bro, you up? I need to tell you something before it hits the gossip vines.

Clint: About to hit the sack. It's bedtime here in Japan. What's up?

Blake: I married Hope this morning.

Clint: AGAIN?

Blake: I know. I KNOW. It was for an alpaca—you know what? Never mind. Just—it would be really awesome if you were here when I break the news to the family.

Clint: Alpaca?

Blake: Did you miss the part where I admitted that I miss

my little brother? And that Japan feels like a long way away?

Clint: Japan IS a long way away, dumbass. And speaking of dumbass—you married Hope because of an alpaca? Not because you two finally quit pretending that you hate each other and worked it out between the sheets?

Blake: Hell no. And that's not the kind of support I'm looking for. I need you to quietly sew some seeds of doubt behind my back. Tell Mom and Dad it's a bad idea. Tell Ryan I was drunk. Tell Jace—hell, I don't care what you tell Jace. He won't hear it. Dopey asshole.

Clint: That's sleep deprivation from having a baby. Which reminds me—you want in on the pool on whether Ryan and Cassie get pregnant before Christmas?

Blake: NO. Can we get through my marriage crisis first?

Clint: Fine. I'll ask again next week. Back to you and Hope. Was it a shotgun wedding?

Blake: No. It was more like...blackmail.

Clint: You threatened to steal her alpaca if she didn't do you the honor of becoming your lawfully wedded wife?

Blake: NO! SHE blackmailed ME, asshole.

Clint: Why? And how? She say she'd set fire to your grape vines?

Blake: No.

Clint: She found those toddler pictures of you from your punk rocker phase? With your little pink and blue mohawk?

Blake: Fine, forget support. Can you just please NOT say "AGAIN" when everyone texts you to find out what you knew about the wedding?

Clint: Have I let it slip in the last four years that you did Vegas the way god intended? No, I haven't. Am I going to now? Well, that depends on how much you lie to me in the next five minutes.

Blake: I'm not lying. We're married. Legally. That's all you need to know.

Clint: Do you love her?

Blake: *middle finger emoji*

Clint: That's not an actual answer, and it could mean yes or no.

Blake: Point is, it won't last. But this time everyone knows, so help me prepare them for the heartbreak of my divorce in three months, okay?

Clint: Hmmm... Mom and Pop really love Hope, you know. Especially after all those nice things she said when she offi- ciated Jace and Olivia's wedding. And isn't Cassie in a book club with her or something?

Blake: They've been volunteering at bingo together, and this is NOT HELPING.

Clint: You could just try to stay married this time.

Blake: SHE HATES MY GUTS.

Clint: Probably because you're always pulling her pigtails. Women hate that. And rightfully so. You like her, tell her you like her.

Blake: She's the one who demanded the annulment in Vegas, not me. She doesn't think I'm marriage material, except when she needs something.

Clint: But you went along with it AGAIN, Mr. "Marriage is for Love." So clearly you see an opportunity here.

Blake: An opportunity to make her as miserable as she makes me.

Clint: Not buying it, bro. You're secretly hoping it works out.

Blake: She short-circuited the entire courthouse and broke three iPhones by looking at them wrong before the ceremony was over.

Clint: Olivia says she needs to get laid to calm the wiper vibes. You're up, husband. Get in there and do your duty.

Blake: This isn't helping.

Clint: You've known me how many years, and you honestly expected help?

Blake: *middle finger emoji*

Clint: You and Hope have been at each other's throats since you both came home from that Vegas trip, which is stupid, because you're perfect for each other. The only problem I see is that you gave up on things too soon.

Blake: That's a pretty fucking big problem.

Clint: And yet, you just married her again, genius. You want my advice, here you go: give it a shot. A real shot.

Blake: Even though we can't stand each other half the time?

Clint: You remember when I destroyed your volcano science fair project in seventh grade?

Blake: Yeah, that sucked, but watching it float down the river was pretty funny.

Clint: EXACTLY. You don't give two shits when people fuck up, unless it affects your business or unless it's Hope. There's something there that you need to work out. Work it out and get your marriage on the right track.

Blake: Our marriage is about protecting her alpaca. That's the track. The only track.

Clint: Keep telling yourself that. And send pictures when

you go see your wifey for conjugal visits. I miss that furball. And by furball, I mean Chewpaca. Not Hope. Obviously.

Blake: Nah, he hates pictures. Shit. I just wrote that. About an alpaca. WHAT THE FUCK IS WRONG WITH ME?

Clint: Unresolved issues, bro. Go work them out. I'm hitting the sack. I expect to hear you're madly in love when I get up in the morning.

Blake: Not gonna happen.

Clint: *chicken emoji*

Blake: And yet somehow I still miss you. I must be out of my mind. Sweet dreams, asshole.

FOUR

Hope

I'm still jittery from Blake's kiss a half hour later, when I pull up at Gram's attorney's office outside of Happy Cat.

I'm blaming it on the fish smell that we waded through to get out of the courthouse. Apparently someone installed an unauthorized microwave under their desk and tried to heat up cod for a mid-morning snack while someone else was burning popcorn in the breakroom and now Happy Cat's courthouse qualifies to be on a food disaster show.

I've been cleared of all wrongdoing for the blown fuses, but my conscience is starting to poke me like Kyle used to in the car when Gram would take us to Atlanta for mandatory finishing school lessons.

Poke poke poke.

You made a good man marry you for an alpaca.

You could be preventing him from meeting the love of his life.

Just because you don't have a desire to be trapped in a doomed marriage doesn't mean he feels the same.

Poke poke poke.

I pull myself out of my ancient Ford pickup—it has fewer electronic systems than modern vehicles and breaks down less than a newer model would—and I head over to rap on the window of Blake's truck.

He holds up a finger while his thumbs dance over his phone screen.

Can fingers be handsome?

Because my temporary husband has *very* handsome fingers.

Fingers that coaxed multiple O's from me multiple times on our first wedding night, taking me to places I'd never been before. Or since.

I sigh.

We could've had such an amazing friends-with-benefits relationship if I hadn't screwed it up by suggesting we hit the Little Chicken Chapel for a quickie wedding.

Further proof that marriage only ends in misery.

Ask my parents. My grandparents. My aunts and uncles and cousins.

If I'm related to them, they have awful marriages.

And if there's one other thing I know about awful marriages, it's that they make for miserable, scared children. Especially children who accidentally short out televisions and Wi-Fi routers and can't stop no matter how angry their parents get or how hard they try.

That's part of the reason I love animals so much.

Animals are easy, innocent, uncomplicated.

Not like humans, who are so often a stress-laced mystery to me...

Blake slides out of his truck in one smooth motion,

phone going to his pocket, arm muscles flexing, his face shrouded in an enigmatic scowl.

"Truck didn't break down this time," he says with a nod to my old beater. "That a first?"

"Nope," I say with a tight smile, determined to make the best of this. I motion toward the front of the Victorian mansion. "Shall we? So I can save an alpaca and you can get your winery off the ground?"

I lead him inside the stately old home that serves as Colton J. Ashford, Esquire's office building. I have a love-hate relationship with this room, a place I've only visited when dealing with something to do with my grandmother's illness or death. Velvet couches, Turkish rugs, original wood floors, and paintings of Victorian-era children hanging on the walls give it a perfectly period feel.

Not a thing is out of place.

It looks so warm and welcoming, like my parents' house.

But this room has one thing going for it that my parents' house never had—an aura of kindness. For all my grandma's faults, she managed to find a very good attorney with a delightful staff.

Like Rae, the sweet receptionist, who glances up as we enter, sweeps an appraising look over my wedding gown, and immediately mutters, "Uh-oh."

She manages to add a sympathetic smile that makes me feel like I've been wrapped in a friendly hug, but I don't miss the way she subtly pulls the phone closer to her as I approach.

I sigh again.

I'd like to say that what happened to the phone system —and the lights—at the reading of Gram's will a few days ago wasn't my fault, except...it was.

"Hi, Rae. Is Mr. Ashford in?"

She touches her hair and peeks at the tall door behind her carved mahogany desk, then rises with a smile. "Hope St. Claire, who is this delicious drink of a man?" she asks instead of answering me.

Blake smiles at her, because he smiles at everyone who's not me, and he reaches over the desk to shake her hand. "Blake O'Dell. Rae, is it? Love the necklace."

"Blake's my husband," I say as Rae's hand goes to the grape pendant dangling from a simple chain around her neck. "We got married over in Happy Cat, so I need to—" I break off as a familiar voice filters from behind the closed office door. I frown. "Is that Kyle in with Mr. Ashford? He's not here to talk about Gram's will, is he?"

"So you already got married?" Rae asks.

"Already married," I confirm. "An hour ago. In Happy Cat."

"Hence the dress," Blake says.

She smiles at him, takes in his dirt-streaked jeans wrapped around his powerful thighs, work boots, and the way his simple gray tee shirt is molding to his chest.

Or maybe that's me noticing how his clothes fit, and she's just wondering why I'd be in a dress while he looks like he was out plowing the fields.

By hand.

Getting dirty.

So, *so* dirty.

Maybe I should've negotiated conjugal rights during this minor prison sentence.

"So why is Kyle here?" I repeat.

"I'm just going to have a quick word with Mr. Ashford," Rae says. "You two sit. I'll order cupcakes from down the road too. So much to celebrate! All this love in the air."

She knocks quickly, then ducks into Mr. Ashford's office, while I crane my neck to see inside.

Kyle *is* in there!

With a *woman*. Wearing a white hat that looks like it has a veil attached.

"Oh, shit," I whisper. My heart fires like I'm on a ten-mile run, and I break out in a cold sweat.

If he got married already...

But he *just met her*. On *Tinder*.

Like five days ago. How can this possibly be happening?!

I need a paper bag.

If he beat me to it—if he got married first—Chewpaca is doomed.

Doomed!

"Hope?" Blake asks.

"My phone," I whisper. "My phone is in my truck."

The lamp on the table beside the velvet couch flickers, and Blake grabs me by the shoulders, sending more goose-bumps prickling across my skin, and guides me to the center of the room, away from anything electrical. "Why do you need your phone?"

"To call Olivia and ask her to go hide Chewpaca. Because if Kyle's in there and he's already married—"

His eyes go wide, but before he can respond, the door swings open, and Rae beckons us. "Come on in, you crazy lovebirds," she says with a smile that's both panicked and genuine. "What a great reason to have a problem!"

I charge into the office so fast I only belatedly realize Blake might not have followed. But when I glance back, he's there, right behind me as Rae closes us into the office, his brows drawing tight, lips thin, eyes flashing at the sight of

Kyle in a suit, holding hands with a red-headed, white-hat-with-veil-wearing stranger.

She's pretty, with freckles, big green eyes, and a chest smaller than his usual, and she's watching us with obvious caution.

"Hope!" Mr. Ashford rises from his desk. He's only in his fifties, but has been silver up top for over a decade. "Rae tells me you got married this morning as well."

My heart sinks to my toes, dragging all of my other organs with it. I think my stomach gets snarled up somewhere near my femur. "As well?"

"We were just finishing up Kyle and Cara's ceremony."

"Just finishing?" My heart rockets back into my chest again. "Oh, well, good! We've been married for over an hour!"

"What? To this asshole?" Kyle demands, jabbing a thumb at Blake.

He looks just like his father—so lanky he can eat whatever he wants and still be on the slim side, a jawbone that could use more definition, and wide-set eyes that skew bulgy even when he's not angry.

I tap my finger to my lip, asking in a syrupy sweet voice, "When a dick calls a real man an asshole, is that a compliment?"

"You hate him," Kyle growls.

"Fine line between love and hate, man." Blake shrugs. "Turns out we like it on this side better."

Casting him a grateful glance, I push the temporary marriage certificate across Mr. Ashford's desk. "We got married first."

Mr. Ashford picks it up and studies it while Kyle glares at me.

"It's not a legit marriage if you don't love him," he says.

"First of all, my marriage is none of your business beyond what it gives me rights to in Gram's will," I say as calmly as I can manage. "And secondly, the will said *married*. That's it. Not humping like bunnies since you met five days ago."

"Actually, I make love more like a giraffe," Cara says.

We all turn and look at her.

She shrugs. "If that's part of the disclosure process or whatever, then I thought it might be relevant."

"You're a beautiful giraffe," Kyle tells her absently while he leans over Mr. Ashford's shoulder. "All neck. I'll suck on it later. Be quiet for now, okay, honey?"

"Kyle's hung like an elephant." She beams. "A honeymoon safari is the perfect choice to celebrate our love."

I gape at her.

Kyle ignores her.

She slides me a wink, and I don't know if it's a *we got married for the will too, and I'm having fun fucking with you* wink, or if it's a *don't you wish your husband was hung like mine* wink, but either way, I suspect I shouldn't underestimate her.

"What do you do when you're not being a giraffe?" Blake asks.

"Quit talking to my wife," Kyle snaps. "Colton, this is bullshit. Their marriage isn't valid for legal purposes because it's not *real*."

"It's absolutely real."

Whoa.

That wasn't me talking.

That was Blake. And he sounded pretty darn convincing.

He wraps his arm around my shoulders and tugs me tight against his side, making me wonder if vaginas can get goosebumps too? Because there's definite tingling going on in my lady parts.

"It's real," Blake says, "and I don't give a damn who got married first. Hope and me? We're destined to be together. So the word you're looking for is *congratulations*. Go ahead. I'll wait."

I squeak out a small breath, because I can't breathe with him gripping me this tight, and also, that may be the sweetest thing anyone's ever said about me.

Except for the part where I can read between the lines, just like I could during his vows.

Destined to be together?

More like destined to make each other miserable, despite the foolishly optimistic thoughts my vagina is currently having.

"I'm going to need time to do some research and consult a few colleagues," Mr. Ashford says with a frown. "This is... highly unusual, to say the least."

"You can either declare me the rightful owner of my grandmother's estate, or you can see us in court," Kyle growls.

In court.

Fighting a legal battle that could take months.

Or years.

Because if we're going to court, Kyle won't stop until he's appealed as high as he can appeal. And so long as Chewpaca's well-being hangs in the balance, I damn well won't stop either, even though I don't have the resources my evil cousin has. I cut ties with the family money years ago.

If only cutting ties with the baggage was as easy.

"There's no reason to go to court," I say, with as much bravado as I can muster. "I was married first. Seems pretty clear cut to me."

"It's my turn to have the llama," he declares. "I want it at my house in two hours."

"He's an *alpaca*," I snap back, "and he's in a good home right now, which is where he'll stay until a court of law orders me to give him up."

"Colton—" Kyle starts, but Mr. Ashford holds a hand up.

"Until the will is fully executed, the estate is handled as the trust dictated. Ms. St. Claire—"

"Mrs. O'Dell," Blake corrects.

I twitch, but force a smile. "Mrs. O'Dell," I agree, even though something deep inside me howls in protest at the name, feeling more stressed out by this arrangement with every passing second.

"*Mrs. O'Dell*, then," Mr. Ashford replies, "I trust you'll continue to care for all of the estate's animals as though they were your own?"

The idea that I'd do anything less is insulting. "*All* animals are well-cared for at my sanctuary *regardless* of where they came from or where they're going."

"Very well, then. Give me some time to look into the precedent in cases like these, and I'll be in touch." He settles back at his desk, then glances up. "Oh. And congratulations and many happy returns to one and all."

"You are going *down*," Kyle mutters while he pushes past me, dragging Cara along with him.

"Watch how you talk to my wife," Blake growls at his back.

I get a happy tingle at the base of my spine, regardless of all the growing evidence that Gram's will is going to do for my life what it took forty years of marriage to do to hers: Slowly shrivel away in a stew of bitterness and anger fueled by box wine she made her chef pour into a Barolo

Monfortino Riserva bottle she kept on hand to keep up appearances.

But seriously, she knew what her grandson was like.

"I can't believe she gave Kyle this kind of opening," I say, turning back to Mr. Ashford. "Didn't she love her alpaca at all?"

He clears his throat and slides his chair closer to his desk. "I believe she wished to know that her bloodline would continue. And she wasn't sure it would without a nudge."

Fabulous.

My grandmother wants to manage my sex life from the grave.

I know even less about how to be a good parent than I do about how to be a good wife, and now I've sucked Blake freaking O'Dell into an endless void of court battles.

He'll probably divorce me before the week is out, once he realizes the kind of fight we're in for, one that definitely won't be over in the three months I promised him.

"I'll be in touch as soon as I've verified the proper legal precedent," Mr. Ashford tells us.

As we head through the lobby, my shoulders are sagging, and the dress I snagged off the rack at Goodwill this morning is starting to let off a funky odor.

Rae tosses paperclips at our feet. "Since I couldn't find rice or birdseed," she explains. "Cara loved it. Such a sweet woman."

A sweet woman who's unwittingly extended an ugly battle for an alpaca that just wants to be loved and left in peace.

I adopted a second alpaca not long after Chewpaca moved to my sanctuary last year, because alpacas can die of loneliness. Chewpaca and Too-Pac are very best buds. It would be criminal to separate them, but Kyle's already made it clear he only wants the alpaca with the perfect pedigree.

It's the St. Claire way.

"Sorry," I mutter to Blake when we're out in the sunshine, which is stupidly bright and happy, showing no respect for all the bad news busting out all over the place.

A few feet away, a VW bug with a giant cupcake on top whips into the last parking spot and a tiny, black-haired woman with an angel face and a sour expression that matches my mood springs out, a pink box propped on her hip. I'd heard there was a new bakery in town, but I hadn't yet met the owner.

"You Rae?" the woman asks. "The one who ordered the wedding cupcakes?" Her eyes are haunted in a way that makes me wonder if her feelings on marriage are similar to my own.

I point to the door. "Rae's inside."

"But we'll take a cupcake if you're sharing," Blake says, only for the sparrow of a person to cut him off with a frantic swipe of her hand.

"Probably best not to touch them," she says. "At least not until I get them inside the building. I've been having some bad delivery luck lately. Very bad..." And with that ominous declaration, she plods across the gravel and up the steps, leaving a sweet and sad scent in her wake, like a sugar-flavored raincloud.

Blake frowns and shrugs, before turning his attention back to me. "So did the will say you have to be married *with kids* to inherit the estate?"

"No. Just married. It didn't even say *happily* married."

We approach my truck, but I can't look at him. I've gone out of my way *not* to like him since we both landed back in

Happy Cat, and now he's stuck in this mess because of me. I have to let him get back to whatever work he was doing before I texted him about a job while I go find another attorney, since odds are good Kyle will take me to court, and I need someone who's firmly on my side rather than the attorney still representing my grandmother's interests.

But I weirdly don't want to say goodbye. And Blake weirdly doesn't seem inclined to head anywhere else.

In fact, as we approach the truck, he boxes me in against the driver's door.

"What are you doing?" I hiss.

"Your dear dick of a cousin is sitting in his car ten feet away," Blake murmurs, leaning close enough for his nose to brush against mine, setting off a fireworks display across the surface of my skin. "He's watching us. So if his argument is going to be that we're not happily married, we'd better put on a good show."

FIVE

Blake

I've lost my damn mind.

I know it was still squirming around in my skull when I got up this morning, but ever since I saw Hope in that wedding dress, everything is short-circuiting, and now, the only thing I can think about is kissing her again.

I keep telling myself I hate Hope St. Claire, but the truth is, the only thing I hate about her is that she doesn't want me.

But right now?

Right now, she's stuck with me.

And we need to put on a good show.

And so I glide my lips over hers, because her cousin *is* watching, and because we both want this. Bad. Within seconds, we're in the same situation as in the dark in the courthouse.

Her fingers are hooking into my belt loops.

Her lips are parting.

The roots of my hair are tingling like I'm inches from a live electrical wire, but all I want to do is get closer. If I'm going to short out, kissing this woman is a hell of a way to go.

The sun beats down on us as she scrapes her teeth over my lower lip and presses her hips into my rapidly hardening cock, which isn't behaving itself like I told it to.

Of course it's not behaving.

Hope St. Claire is the sexiest woman I've ever known in my life.

Much as I've tried to deny it the last four years, it's true. She's all passion and heart and I'm a sucker for both.

"Is he still watching?" she breathes against my mouth.

"Yes. Definitely."

I angle my mouth and trace kisses from the corner of her mouth to her ear, and then down to her jaw, her skin like honey on my lips.

"If I didn't know better, I'd think you were trying to get into my pants," she murmurs through soft gasps while she hooks one leg behind mine, trapping me in yards of satin and that fluffy white netting stuff that makes her look like she's sitting on a cloud of cotton candy.

"You're not wearing pants," I reply. "Problem solved. Are you wearing underwear? No, don't tell me. Don't ruin the fantasy."

"Quit fantasi—*oh*."

I suckle harder on her neck just below her ear, and she shifts to spread her legs and straddle my thigh.

"This—isn't—"

"Shh. The sooner we get you that llama, the better for both of us."

"*Alpaca*."

I know it's an alpaca, but she gets pissed when I call it a

llama, and I need her to get pissed.

I need to have a reason to stop kissing her neck.

The truck metal is hot, but if I move my hands to touch her, I'm going to get arrested for public indecency.

I've waited four years to touch Hope again.

Hell if I'll be able to stop myself from touching all of her.

Her breasts.

Her hips.

Her pussy.

"He's driving away," she gasps.

The purr of an expensive car engine fading away confirms that we don't have to keep kissing.

But she's not blowing up circuits or griping at me for baiting her or tempting me by smiling so brightly at one of her rescue dogs that I want to throw her over my shoulder, march her to the barn, and kiss her until she admits she still has feelings for me.

But I *am* kissing her.

And maybe if I keep it up, she'll see she's been wrong, that she never should have walked out on me that steamy morning in Vegas.

"*Blake*. Stop." She pushes at my shoulders, and I pull back. "We're not doing this," she adds in a shaky voice.

I lift a brow. "Being married?"

Her gaze darts to the attorney's office. "Meet me at my place at seven. I need to get home and make sure all the chores are done around the sanctuary. And you need— something, probably."

A cold shower?

Yes.

I have a dozen things on my to-do list, but first, a cold shower.

SIX

Hope

I'm mucking the goat stalls when I hear a familiar voice.

"Hello? Hope? Are you in there, lovely?"

"Olivia! Come in!" I set the shovel against the rough wooden wall and turn to wave at my favorite California girl. The willowy blonde has a little bundle of joy tucked into a sling on the front of her chest and is beaming in the way only Olivia can, with sunshine radiating out her pores and her presence bringing peace to all humble peasants like me.

And she's not alone. "Cassie!"

The shorter brunette smiles at me as well, and I go momentarily speechless as the reality of my situation sets in.

These two are married to Blake's brothers, which means...

We're sisters for real now. At least for a little while.

"Is it true?" Cassie bounces on her toes, making her glasses slip. She pushes them back up her nose with a giddy grin. "Did you and Blake really elope this morning at the courthouse?"

The gossip took longer than it probably should have to reach them, which I'm guessing means Blake didn't call his family to tell them the bad news—I mean, *happy* news as soon as we left Mr. Ashford's office.

"I—we—yeah," I say awkwardly, biting my bottom lip. I should have thought of how to handle this, but I haven't. Before running into Kyle at the lawyer's office, I would have just told both of my besties the truth, but now...

Cassie and Olivia both squeal, and suddenly I'm enveloped in a girlfriend hug.

Tears sting my eyes, both because these two have become so dear to me over the past year, and also because I know they're going to hate me when Blake and I break up in a few months.

"You should've called us," Cassie says.

"Your auras are so compatible, even when you fight," Olivia adds with a happy sigh. "Sometimes fighting is the best foreplay, don't you think? I'm going to pick a fight with Jace when I get home in your honor."

Cassie laughs. "How did he propose?"

"Was it magical?" Olivia asks, her words practically sparkling in the sunshine.

"I would say I can't believe you're mucking stalls on your wedding day," Cassie adds. "But of course you are."

"We can't wait to throw you a reception." The baby squirms in the sling between us, and Olivia pulls back to coo at her. "We all want to celebrate their joy. Don't we, darling girl? Yes, we do."

Cassie stares at me expectantly, her big blue eyes warm and excited. "I heard you were sitting on the courthouse steps in a wedding dress and there were dandelions involved and then Blake showed up. That's all the gossip I've managed to score so far, so spill it, woman!"

"Well, I..." I shrug, wheels frantically turning, but no explanation pops to mind, so I stall. "I've always loved dandelions. They were originally called lion's tooth because they're so tough they can grow almost anywhere. They thrive even when people do their best to weed them out. That always spoke to me, so I decided when I was twelve that they were the flower for me."

I *do* love dandelions. But even at twelve, I knew marriage wasn't in my genes.

Olivia nods while this year's batch of baby goats bleat in excitement in their pen behind me, knowing it's getting close to pasture frolic time. "That's lovely. And just like a dandelion, you and Blake are ready to thrive together."

I wince, but thankfully neither of them notices.

"But why didn't you tell us you were finally seeing each other?" Cassie asks. "You know we *can* keep secrets, right? Even Baby Clover Dawn."

Olivia nods seriously and cradles the infant through the sling. "She's very good at secrets. And she will continue to be. Secret-keeper is written all over her star chart."

"Well, I... Um, I..." I trail off, uncertain what to say next, and turn to check on the goats instead. Because goats are simple and uncomplicated and everything I need right now.

"Hope?" Cassie says gently. "This *is* a good thing, isn't it? You and Blake?"

"Of course. I'm just nervous because no one in my family has ever done marriage right," I blurt. "So I'm probably going to screw it all up."

"There's no one right formula for marriage," Cassie tells me gently.

"It's true," Olivia agrees. "Every relationship is unique."

"But my ancestors were trying to poison each other with mutual marital animosity on their way over on the Mayflower," I say. "A trend the St. Claires of recent generations have totally embraced. I have literally never seen a healthy relationship up close."

Cassie's lips part, but before she can speak the dogs start barking outside, a warning chorus that makes it clear whoever's approaching isn't a friend. But it's not a stranger, either. The Stranger Danger bark is deeper, sharper.

I excuse myself, moving out of the barn in time to see my cousin picking his way across the lawn in his three-hundred-dollar loafers, the expression on his face making it obvious that he's revolted by mud, grass, animals, and the possibility of stepping in something natural an animal might have left behind.

This might be the first time those shoes have made contact with anything that wasn't plush carpet, wide-plank wood, or their shrine in Kyle's closet.

Instantly, I break out in an even more intense sweat while I cross the short distance to where the dogs have gathered at the fence line. "Shh. It's okay, Buddy. Good girl, Sunshine. I've got him, Rambo. Good dogs."

But I'm pretty sure he has me, not the other way around.

Plus, I have to get Olivia and Cassie out of here before Kyle throws more doubt on my state of wedded bliss. I can't bear to explain to my friends what a failure I'm going to be in the marriage department. Especially since they're related by marriage to my fake husband.

I duck my head back into the goat barn. "Ugh. Kyle's coming. You guys should dash. Clover doesn't need to breathe in his bad aura."

They both pull faces—even Olivia, who hastily says,

"But maybe she could improve the balance of his heart chakra."

"No, really—I don't want to bring you guys down with his grouchy snootiness."

"You're sure you don't want us to stay for backup?" Cassie asks. "I'm not afraid of jerks, you know."

"Neither are we," Olivia says. "Clover seems to like them, actually. Grouchy people make her giggle." Clover burbles and flashes a gummy grin my way, as if to assure me that she can handle my craptastic cousin.

I smile, because she's the cutest thing I've ever seen without fur and four legs. "No, you guys make a run for it. He's probably here on family business we should discuss privately. And the sooner we start, the sooner he'll leave."

"All right, but call me later," Cassie says, scooting toward the back door. "I've got your back, sister. I'll share all my top-secret tips to a happy marriage with an O'Dell man and you'll feel ready to rock the newlywed thing in no time."

"Me too. And trust the universe. This was written in the stars and the stars don't lie," Olivia says, following Cassie out the back with one last wiggle of her fingers.

"But I apparently lie all the time these days," I mutter, feeling terrible for misleading my best friends, who are meandering over to the pasture to visit with Chewpaca instead of crossing paths with Kyle, while I try to finish mucking the last stall before he reaches me.

Unfortunately, the lying can't be helped. The fewer people who know that my marriage is a sham, the better. At least until Mr. Ashford gets back to us on what the legal precedents are in a case like this.

And my friends will hopefully understand why I've had to be less than truthful. They both love Chewpaca and would be on board with whatever it takes to protect him from falling into the clutches of Kyle the Wretched.

Although they'd probably prefer I hadn't picked *Blake* as a husband, if I had to get married for an alpaca and have no intention of staying that way. Because they both also adore Blake.

Everyone loves Blake.

It's hard not to.

He's a total sweetheart to everyone but me.

"There you are. Figured you'd be up to your elbows in animal feces," Kyle says, his voice dripping with disdain.

"Nope, just up to my knees at the moment," I say with a saccharine grin. "To what do I owe the pleasure? Come to your senses and realized you're unfit to be an alpaca parent?"

He rolls his ice blue eyes. "We *own* animals, Hope. We parent children. There's a difference."

"Not to me," I say, stabbing my shovel into the ground and fisting the handle while behind me Biscuit, Mickey, and Dorito bleat in baby-goat distress at having a big ol' meanie in their home.

"Right. That's why you fry up a half pound of human infant in your skillet every Sunday."

I recoil. "Jesus, Kyle. What's wrong with you?"

"There's nothing wrong with me," he says, his cold eyes as emotionless as ever. "I'm making a logical argument."

"Well, go make it somewhere else. Until Mr. Ashford gets back to us with more information, I don't see that we have anything more to discuss."

"You've always been so short-sighted." He crosses his arms over his chest, his mouth going soft at the edges in a way I haven't seen many times before. Not since we were kids, anyway. "But I need to consider the bigger picture, cousin. Cara really wants to go on safari for our honeymoon. She's got vacation days saved up that she has to use by the end of September, and I'm taking leave from work for the rest of the year until I figure out what I want to do next."

I bite my lip, holding in a taunt about seeing how fast he can spend the trust fund money our grandfather left him. Grandpa was a sexist from way back. When he went into the nursing home a few years ago, he gave Kyle unrestricted access to his accounts. And when he died, he left Kyle, the only male cousin, an obscene amount of money to "help him start a family."

The three girls each got one of *his* grandmother's historically significant quilts. Sabrina and Vivian immediately sold theirs on eBay, and were disinherited from Gram's will as a result.

I donated mine to a museum, and moved on.

I don't resent Kyle for winning the Our Grandfather Thought Women Were Only Good For Being Barefoot and Pregnant lottery, but I sure as heck resent him fighting to get his greedy hands on Chewpaca too.

He already has more than his fair share of resources.

"So you're ceding that I'd be the better alpaca parent since you're unemployed." I smile. "Excellent. I accept."

"I've already picked a breeding facility, and they're prepared to take the animal immediately. They've got several paying customers lined up and waiting."

My throat tightens. "And they'll keep waiting while I see you in court."

He frowns. "A lengthy court battle would cast a pall over our month abroad."

My eyes go wide. "A month?"

"A honeymoon isn't something that should be rushed." He sniffs. "It sets the tone for the entire marriage. Grandpa took Gram to Paris for six weeks when they were first married."

"And look how great that turned out," I mutter.

"They were together for fifty years."

"But miserable for at least half of it."

"Not everyone needs to be *happy* all the time, Hope. Your view on marriage is so bourgeoisie," he says with a sigh. "Blake would probably be a great fit for you. Too bad you're faking it."

"I am not," I say, lifting my chin. "We're ridiculously in love."

"You are not, and as soon as my attorney proves it, we'll be taking possession of the stud." He smirks like it's his job. And maybe it is—I can't see that he's done much else since he quit his investment firm last year. "He tells me that because we were both married on the same day, we can either agree to split the estate, or the courts can decide whose marriage is more valid."

"Great. Leave me the animals, and you can have everything else."

"Cara and I don't want everything else. We want the alpaca. And we're going to get it before we leave for our honeymoon next month."

I narrow my eyes. "You really expect me to believe the courts will think you're madly in love with a woman you met five days ago on Tinder? What about the validity of your marriage? Why isn't that in question?"

"Or we could settle this out of court so my bride can have the honeymoon of her dreams," he counters. "If that doesn't prove she's my top priority, I don't know what will."

"All it proves is that you have money to spend and like to travel with female companionship."

"You can keep the rest of the animals. Hell, take the

house and farm too. Sign the alpaca over to me, and we all walk away happy."

"Chewpaca wouldn't be happy."

"I'm trying to offer you the easy out, Hope. Take my offer, or I'll have to prove to the courts that you're faking your marriage. And I *will* prove it before I leave for my honeymoon." He sniffs. "Probably sooner. Since we both know it's a sham."

I chew on the inside of my cheek. Maybe Kyle and Cara *are* in love. I thought I was in love once, and it struck me out of the blue.

If he's right—if the courts will determine who gets Chewpaca based on whose marriage is most valid, then I'm in trouble.

But if I can stall him while I find my own attorney who can argue that I have Chewpaca's best interests at heart—and an established history of quality care—then maybe we have a chance.

I just have to fake my marriage for a little while longer.

A month, tops.

I can do anything for a month.

I could sleep on a bed of nails for that long.

Live in a straw hut filled with fire ants.

Keep my nails nicely painted with no chips in the polish and remember to lift my pinkie every time I take a sip of my morning coffee.

Okay, maybe not that last one, but surely, I can make being married to Blake look like the real thing for a month.

As if summoned by my thoughts, I hear Blake's pickup rumble onto the gravel parking lot by the house. Instantly, the dogs launch into their excited *welcome* bark, because they love Blake.

Naturally.

I decide to take it as a sign that my new husband is riding in to my rescue.

Or that he's come to completely destroy my attempts to prove our marriage is legal, but a little optimism never hurt anyone.

"I don't have any clue how you think you can judge a marriage to be a sham or not." I meet Kyle's gaze and hold it without wavering. "Marriages are all unique."

Or so say Cassie and Olivia, and I trust them.

"It'll be simple," Kyle says, clearly unimpressed with my argument. "We'll ask Ruthie May to be the final judge of any and all evidence procured. She's a shameless gossip, but she always has her facts straight."

That shouldn't be a terrifying idea, but he's not wrong. "Fine. But she likes me more than you."

"Everyone likes you more," Kyle says with a disinterested shrug. "This isn't a popularity contest. It's the sanctity of small-town gossip at stake. Ruthie May will tell the truth, even if it hurts."

Again, he's not wrong.

"But she'll be gossiping about *your* marriage too," I point out.

"I'm unconcerned. Cara and I are deeply in love. But since gossip isn't always admissible in court—though Ruthie May's should be—I also have a backup plan."

Blake appears in the entrance to the barn, making the hairs on the back of my neck stand on end.

"So what's so special about seven o'clock, St. Claire? And who's the creep parked across the street?" he asks in a decidedly unromantic voice, before his gaze lands on Kyle and his lips curve into a tight smile. "Hey, there. Didn't realize you had company, sugar lips."

Sugar lips? We really need to work on his pet name

choices, but first to undo any damage that grouchy tone might have inflicted.

"I missed you, baby!" Letting my shovel fall to the ground, I dash across the dirt-streaked concrete to jump into his arms. He catches me as easily as if he's done it a hundred times before, making my pulse pick up and my voice breathier as I add, "Kyle wants to settle this estate thing before he leaves for his honeymoon in a month, but he thinks he's going to do it by proving we're not really in love. Isn't that the funniest?"

"Totally." Blake's smile widens, but I'm close enough to see the fear flicker in his deep green eyes.

But this isn't the time for fear. It's time to be bold, confident, and commit fully to faking it until we make it. Chewpaca's future well-being depends on it.

I press my lips to Blake's, funneling all the passion I feel for my animals into the kiss, only to have Chewpaca, and just about everything else, banished from my mind by the chemistry that ignites between us every time we touch.

Way too many seconds later, I finally rip my mouth from his, breathless and buzzing all over, to hear Kyle slow-clapping as he circles around us, heading for the exit.

"Nice performance, but it's going to take more than a conveniently timed make-out session to win." He grins. "See you soon, and remember, I've got my eye on you." Shifting his attention to Blake, he adds, "Oh, and the creep across the street is a private detective I've hired to monitor your every move until you screw up. Good luck keeping up the façade twenty-four seven, losers. I give you two days, three tops. Chewpaca will be mine before next Sunday."

"Not going to happen," I call after him.

But I don't sound as sure of myself as I'd like, and when I turn back to Blake, his smile has gone rueful at the edges.

"You realize what this means, right?" he asks.

"That we can probably get that divorce sooner than we thought?" I whisper, flashing two thumbs up. "As soon as the paperwork is final, and Kyle and Cara leave on their honeymoon safari? We can fake this for a month, right?"

"It means one of us needs to get busy packing our bags, pumpkin," he says. "Because if there's one thing happily married people like to do, it's live together."

I lift startled eyes to him, because did he just say he's in this all the way? "Live together? As in under the same roof? You and me? Together?"

"You want to save that alpaca or not?"

"Shit," I mutter, making Blake's grin stretch wider.

Of course I want to save Chewpaca.

But shacking up with Blake?

There's no way I can live with him and not do something I'll regret. It's not a question of *if* I'll throw myself at his body, vagina first, but when.

And then saving Chewpaca might not be the question.

The question might be saving *me*.

SEVEN

Blake

We walk back to my truck hand-in-hand after chasing an aggressive peacock out of the dog pen while I try to not panic.

Move in together?

This will either be the best or the worst idea I've ever had.

I seem to be full of those today. Or at least surrounded by them.

Hope is wearing a smile so stiff it wouldn't fool a blind man in the dark, but hopefully the creep parked in an ancient Ford station wagon by the pasture on the other side of the road will think we're acting weird because we're being watched.

And photographed.

And waved at like we're all old friends.

And now the slim man, dressed in head-to-toe khaki,

with an old school camera hanging around his neck and a neatly trimmed moustache straight out of the Roaring Twenties, is limping across the road and the shelter's gravel parking lot to meet us. "Hey, y'all. Dean Finister. Kind of an odd spot we're in, but it's great to meet you."

Hope starts to extend her hand, but I circle my fingers lightly around her wrist and draw it to my chest. In testimony to how shell-shocked she is by the day's events, she doesn't even try to pull away or order me to quit bossing her around.

"I'm sure you'll understand if we're not prepared to make nice with you, Dean," I say in a firm but civil tone. He'll get the mean voice if he doesn't get off Hope's property once he's asked. I hate the mean voice, but it's necessary sometimes. "We value our privacy and don't appreciate strangers in our business."

"Especially strangers who are trying to prove we don't love each other." Hope wraps her arms around my waist and melts against my side. I hug her closer, because we're trying to fool this nosy bastard and because it feels good.

Mostly because it feels good.

"Oh, I hear you," Dean says, expression sobering. "It's an ugly business sometimes, detective work. But there aren't many jobs that are a good fit for a former cop with a bum knee." He pats his right leg. "Took a bullet right under my kneecap in a drug bust."

Hope makes a soft, dismayed sound. "I'm so sorry. Thank you for your service."

"Of course. It was my pleasure. Loved being a cop," he says, grinning again. "But since I can't protect and serve anymore, I point and shoot," he continues with a chuckle, lifting his camera into the air. "But this is the one and only time I'll step onto your property. I'll keep my distance and keep this as respectful as I possibly can." His smile stretches even wider, revealing slightly crooked teeth that emphasize the perfectly groomed lines of his moustache. "As soon as I catch you not being in love, I'll turn over what I've got to your cousin and be out of your hair for good. Congratulations, by the way. On your marriage. You're a handsome couple." He holds up his hands, making a rectangle shape with his thumbs and pointer fingers and framing us up. "Like one of those pictures that come with the frame, you know? Almost too pretty to be real."

"But we are real," I insist, beginning to suspect Dean's folksy friendliness is a weapon in his arsenal, a way to convince his prey to drop their guard and spill their secrets. "And we don't want to be your friend, Mr. Finister."

"At least not right now," Hope says, pinching my back through my shirt. "Maybe after you're done investigating us, though? If you're staying in town? We all do our share of fussing in Happy Cat, but we're good at forgiving and forgetting and moving on after."

Dean's eyes wrinkle at the edges. "Haven't decided where I'm settling full-time yet, but thank you, ma'am. I appreciate your kindness." He turns to me, gaze softening. "And I respect your position too, Mr. O'Dell. Back when my Loretta was still alive, there wasn't anything I wouldn't have done to keep her safe and happy."

Hope makes another distressed sound and this time even I feel shitty. Dean may be a master manipulator on a mission to catch us with our fake marriage showing, but there's nothing worse than losing someone you love.

"Sorry for your loss," I say gruffly, extending my hand. "And thanks for your understanding."

"Of course." We shake—firmly, but with mutual respect, no alpha male posturing in the grip—and he backs away with a wave to Hope. "Have a great night. And remember to be good to each other. Being a newlywed can be stressful. Love isn't always as easy as they make it out to be in the movies, you know?"

"Thanks. We will. Goodbye." She returns his wave, waiting until he starts back across the road to his battered station wagon before she turns to face me and whispers, "Was that weird?"

"Dunno. I've never been trailed by a PI before."

"They never introduce themselves in the movies. And how does he think he's going to catch us when he told us he's watching?"

"Maybe it's a ploy to make us relax our guard?"

She shivers. "I don't think he needs it. He's got our number already, doesn't he? I swear I felt like his moustache was looking straight through me."

I arch a brow. "His moustache?"

"My dad had a moustache for most of my childhood. Nothing got by that man or his lip toupee," she says, casting a nervous glance over her shoulder. "I'm very bad at lying to well-groomed facial hair."

I smile. "Then let me do the talking, you can do the snuggling, and we'll be just fine. When did you say Kyle's leaving?"

"In a month."

"Easy. What can go wrong in a month?"

Her eyes widen. "Everything?"

"No. Not everything." I glance over her shoulder to where Dean appears to be reading a book in the driver's seat. But even with his attention fixed on something else, I feel watched and I'm pretty sure every second of this interaction is being scrutinized.

Maybe he's the decoy PI and there's actually someone else watching us too.

Great.

Now I'm getting paranoid. And I suddenly feel a desperate need to go check on my grape vines.

"But don't feel obligated to be friendly to him," I say. "As nice as he might seem, he's not on our side."

"Right," she says, nibbling at her bottom lip.

"What?"

"I just..." She shrugs. "*Our* side. It's strange to hear you say that, to think that we're actually on the same side for once."

"You're my wife," I say, my brow furrowing.

"But not really," she huffs.

"The ceremony was legal. So yes, Hope. Really."

"But it's not the same."

"It's the same to me. I don't take promises lightly, especially promises made in a court of law." I catch her chin lightly in my fingers, tilting her face up to mine. "So until such time as we obtain a divorce, you're my wife, and I will personally destroy anyone who even thinks about fucking with you."

Her eyes narrow. "Except for you, right?"

My mind dives straight between the sheets, imagining all the ways I would love to fuck with Hope as soon as possible, but before I can say something suggestive and make a fool of myself, she adds, "You're still going to do your best to make my life miserable?"

Her words hit me in the gut and the pride with collateral damage to the integrity. Have I really been that awful to her? "I don't try to make you miserable on purpose."

"No?" she asks. "Because I'm the only person in town

that you don't get along with. And it's not like I'm not a nice person. I have friends. I don't cuss around babies or tap dance in church. Animals love me, and animals are very good judges of character. But I blow out one little toaster, and it's all *you can't do anything right, can you, Hope?* Just like my parents."

"Yeah, well you—you *look* at me wrong." Wow. That was lame.

She rolls her eyes.

"Let's just go," she says stiffly. "I need to check on Chewpaca, and the sooner we get your stuff, the sooner we can get you settled in the guest room."

"And that'll look good for our case. People come over and see my shit in your guest room. I'd be better off on the couch. At least that doesn't look like a permanently separate situation."

Plus, last I knew, her tiny guest room was overflowing with all the small appliances she's blown out over the years. If she cleans that right after we got married, people will talk.

She exhales sharply. "Fine. I'll clear out part of the closet and a few drawers in my room for your things., but you're not sleeping in my bed. And you're definitely not doing anything else in my bed, so you can get that out of your head right now."

I snort, forehead wrinkling. "As if I would give you the pleasure. You think way too highly of yourself, St. Claire."

"Felt like you thought pretty highly of me too, when we were kissing by my truck."

I put an arm around her waist, pulling her close as I lean down to whisper in her ear. "There's a private detective watching us right now. You want to keep fighting and screw this up before we even get started? Or do you want to get your sweet ass inside and make dinner while I go get my things?"

"I'm not your little Suzy Homemaker, O'Dell," she says, her tone as sharp as her body is soft and sweet. Her arms go around me as she arches closer, putting on a good show for our spy while she adds, "I have animals to feed and evening chores to finish. If you want dinner tonight you're going to have to make it yourself. My offer was to help you move your shit, not wait on you hand and foot."

"I don't need your help moving my shit." I squeeze her ass in one hand, summoning a hungry sound from her throat that I know pisses her off. She can pretend she doesn't want me, but her body betrays her every time.

She sounds even angrier when she says, "And I don't need a knight in shining armor. You're my pretend husband, that's it. So keep your hands to yourself when you get back. As soon as we're alone, we're operating under the four-foot rule. Meaning there will be at least four feet of distance between us at all times."

I turn my head, nuzzling my lips closer to her ear as I whisper, "You're not making the rules, honey bear. Marriage is a team effort, which means you and I are going to have to learn to work together." I slide my hand beneath her tee shirt, trailing my fingers up the hollow of her spine, wickedly satisfied by the way she shivers in response. "I'll be home by nine. You can leave my plate in the microwave. I'll warm it up after I get my things inside."

"Fuck you," she grits out, making me grin as I pull away.

"Maybe." I wink. "If you're a very good doo-doo-kins."

"Your nicknames are an abomination," she mutters through clenched teeth, wiggling her fingers as I back toward my truck.

"Keep pushing me," I say with a grin. "They can always get worse."

"I hate you." She beams at me.

"Mutual," I lie, saluting her before slamming into my truck and firing it up with a too-rough jerk of my wrist.

I don't hate her, despite the fact that she's right, and I *am* ruder to her than I am to anyone else on earth. But fighting with Hope is more fun than making love to most women.

Maybe I'm a sadist.

I never thought I was the kind of man who got off on punishment, but a month with that woman—being so close to her, so turned on by everything about her, but unable to get within four feet of her unless other people are around—is going to be torture.

And I sort of think I'm looking forward to it.

Yup, I admit it, as I catch myself whistling a jaunty tune while I pack up my clothes and essential items from the cabin. I've been living on Jace's property for the past two years to be closer to my vines as they matured. I'm excited to move in with my nemesis.

And maybe she doesn't hate me as much as she's pretending.

When I get back to the farmhouse with the wraparound porch, Hope is locked in her office with classical music playing at a volume that doesn't invite a knock, but there are a series of sticky notes on the door that read—*The two bottom drawers are yours and I cleared out half of the closet. If you need more space, I'll see what I can do tomorrow. There are sheets and a pillow on the couch for you and a fresh towel in the guest bath.*

See you tomorrow. Thanks for marrying me. You didn't have to, and I appreciate it, even if we have differences of opinion on how a fake marriage should play out.

Oh—and I contacted the other people I asked to get hitched, and told them it was all a ruse to make you wake up and realize that we're meant to be together forever. Hopefully that'll hold up if Dean gets around to talking to any of them. Frederick, my first fake fiancé, lives in Atlanta, and I'm sure he has no plans to return to Happy Cat after I almost murdered his father so we should be safe on that front, too.

Have you been dating anyone recently? Someone we might need to make explanations to or for? Not trying to be nosy, just wanting to make sure we cover all our bases. I obviously don't care one way or another.

And your plate of meatloaf and green beans is in the microwave. They're leftovers from two days ago, though, so don't start thinking you're special.

I smile. "Don't start thinking I'm special," I mutter, as I watch the meatloaf spin in the orange glare inside her pristinely clean microwave that makes my soup-splattered one look like I'm a savage who was raised in a monkey cage.

Don't go thinking I'm special...

But as I eat the homemade meal, by far the best I've had in weeks, I can't help feeling a little special. Her gesture of kindness, even couched in insults, went a long way. Makes me wonder what a bigger gesture could do.

She's right. I need to be nicer to her. It's not her fault electronics blow up when she's around, and while it's technically her fault our Vegas wedding ended in an annulment, how many Vegas weddings last?

And what did she mean, I was *just like her parents*?

I don't know the St. Claires well, but I know Hope.

Well enough anyway.

She's right. Animals adore her, and she adores them right back. She works hard to give them a safe home, and I know she's not doing it with family money.

She earns everything she has, even though she probably doesn't have to.

Cassie and Ryan love her.

Olivia and Jace love her.

Hell, she and Clint barely crossed paths back when we were all in school—he only got to know her at the weddings —and as far as I can tell, he loves her.

So why can't Hope and I get along?

Better yet...why can't we do *more* than get along?

When I saw her in the casino in Vegas that weekend when I was in college, a blast from the past I'd rarely seen since our high school graduation—I was going to school at CalTech and had stayed out west for a summer internship— she was hunched over a slot machine looking like her dog died.

Like *all* of her dogs died.

I wanted to make her smile. I *needed* to make her smile.

I can't finish vet school and my life is over and I don't want to talk about it, but I kinda want to self-destruct, she'd said, tears in those big brown eyes that suddenly seemed even more beautiful than they had when we were just friends growing up.

I offered to sit with her while she waited for her friends to join her the next day.

The slot machine short-circuited.

Casino security asked her to leave.

And I designated myself her personal guardian while we went to a second casino, where she picked the blackjack table and then the roulette wheel—no electronics involved— and we won big and celebrated with too many rum and cokes.

Seven hours later, we were hitched.

Twenty-four after that, we were over.

I never got to romance her. Outside the bedroom, that is.

Maybe this is my second chance.

Hell, no *maybe* about it. Clint's right. This *is* my second chance.

Once again, her life has taken a bad turn, and once again, I'm here.

It's time for me to man up.

Pretend this is real?

Hell, no.

I'm gonna make this real.

Operation: Real Romance, here I come.

EIGHT

Cassie: Hey babes! I hate to interrupt you on your first night of wedded bliss, but George Cooney is having tummy troubles, and I'd really appreciate some expert raccoon advice.

Hope: Hey! I'm no expert, but I'll do my best.

Cassie: You are too an expert. You're totally an animal doctor, just without the official paperwork.

Hope: Ha. Well, the state of Georgia likes official paperwork. And I'm sure there are a lot of things I missed dropping out of school with a year left to go. But I'm happy to try to help.

Cassie: You're sure I'm not bothering you? Cramping your wedding night style?

Hope: Not at all. Blake was so beat from our big day he's already dead to the world. I was just reading to unwind a little. What's up with George?

Cassie: He got into the pantry after dinner, before I put the padlock on the door again, and he ate an entire jar of peanut butter. Now, he's rolling around on the carpet in the living room, moaning and clutching his stomach like he's in pain, while also trying to steal Ryan's popcorn every time he leaves the bowl unattended. He could just be playing up his starvation to score treats after eight p.m., but this feels different than the usual theatrics.

Hope: Hmmm... A jar of peanut butter is a lot. Was it full?

Cassie: Practically. And he licked that sucker clean.

Hope: Did Sticky Fingers get into it too?

Cassie: No, just George. The babies didn't touch it either.

Hope: Aww. That's probably good. I loved the family photo of them you sent last week. Who knew George would be a family man? Although, I guess it makes sense, with you and Ryan as role models. So has he been drinking since the PB encounter?

Cassie: No. I refilled his water dish because I was worried he had peanut butter stuck to the roof of his mouth, but he hasn't touched it.

Hope: Okay. Well, peanut butter is on the approved list of foods for raccoons. In moderation. But it's got a lot of junk in it, too, and wild animals aren't built to process that much refined sugar. Try giving him some ice chips in a bowl. That'll give him something to chew on and get water into him at the same time. I think your best bet is to get him hydrated and keep him on crickets and found-in-nature foods tomorrow. That'll be a fun treat for his family, too. But if he gets worse or you notice increased swelling or tenderness in the abdominal area, you should take him in to the vet.

Cassie: Gotcha. Will do. Thank you so much! Ryan's going to get ice chips now. He said to tell Blake hi, by the way, and that he and Jace are going to take him out for a post-wedding bachelor party as soon as they all have a night off.

Hope: Oh good. I'm sure Blake will love that. But I bet Ryan and Jace are thinking we're crazy people, huh?

Cassie: No, actually, LOL. Ryan didn't seem all that surprised. Jace, either. Guess they know their brother better than the rest of us.

Hope: Wow. Really? They're not just being nice?

Cassie: Remember who we're talking about here, woman. Jace doesn't play nice and Ryan is incapable of hiding anything from me. If he were secretly weirded out, I'd know about it. Oh, and speaking of weird, Savannah signed on for another year with her cranky old English dude, even though he's the worst.

Hope: Another year with his daughter, you mean. It's Beatrice she loves. And living in England. And clotted cream.

Cassie: *drooling emoji* Omg, clotted cream. It's almost enough to convince me to cross the pond for good. And lemon curd. And scones. And I know I'm in the minority here, but I love their gorgeous bloody breakfasts, complete with meat feast and grilled mushrooms and tomatoes and beans on the side. I mean, why not have beans for breakfast?

Hope: I'm totally open to beans for breakfast. Upon occasion.

Cassie: Me too. And I was open to Savannah nannying while she took the time she needed to heal from her divorce, but the clock is ticking. Beatrice is a treasure of a kid and I absolutely adore her, but I can't help feeling like my sister's signing over her life to this guy, a piece at a time. She's still young, but she's not that young. And if she's spending all of her time taking care of another man's child, she's not getting any closer to having a family of her own. Meanwhile, Stuffy Old Colin could fire her at any time and she'd be cut off from Beatrice and her heart would be broken into a zillion little pieces again. I hate to think that way, but I can't help it. And also I just...want her living close again. Is that awful?

Hope: It's not awful. I can imagine I'd feel the same way. But you have to trust that Savannah's making the best decision for her, even if you would choose differently in her place.

Cassie: You're right. You're so sweet and wise, you know that? Way beyond your years. And I love that I can trust you to give me an honest opinion, even when you know it's not what I want to hear.

Hope: Thanks, but...you'd forgive me if I messed up someday, right? And did something not entirely sweet or wise?

Cassie: Of course I would, but you have to stop worrying about you and Blake, okay? If it gets screwed up, you won't have screwed it up alone. It takes two to make a thing go wrong too. And yeah, you and Blake came out of nowhere for some of us, but a lot of people have seen this coming a mile away. Take comfort in that—and your cute new hubby —and relax. Everything's going to work out for the best. It almost always does, especially when you're putting love first.

Hope: Okay. Love you. Give me an update on George in the morning okay?

Cassie: Will do. And love you too. I may not have my blood sister here, but I'm lucky enough to have you and Olivia, so I really shouldn't complain. *winking emoji* See you at bingo tomorrow night. Sleep well!

NINE

Hope

I do not sleep well.

I'm up most of the night, plagued by crazy dreams, guilt over lying to Cassie and the people I care about, a hyperactive awareness of the sexy-as-sin man sacked out on my couch—with the blinds pulled in case the detective tries to sneak photos in the middle of the night—and the very real terror that if I fall asleep I will wake up to find I have sleepwalked myself on top of him and am making out with his stupid face.

And I will *not* make out with his stupid face in private.

Any kissing that takes place will be for the benefit of Kyle and his spies. And I most certainly won't let Blake O'Dell get me all tingly again or give him any other reason to think this marriage is real enough to warrant his protection or devotion.

Admittedly, hearing him vow to annihilate my enemies was insanely hot, but it was also scary.

I'm not ready to be anyone's wife for real, and I don't know that I ever will be.

It's like I grew up in that scary hotel from *The Shining*, and now someone's asking me to move into a building that looks *exactly* like that one and get snowed in for the rest of my life.

It'll be fine, they say. *No ghosts or demons or blood in the elevators or creepy twins this time around, and absolutely no one will go insane and try to kill you with an ax.*

They're probably right, but I'm still not setting foot in that hotel anytime soon.

Maybe ever.

It's a relief when my alarm goes off at five. Now I can get up and get out of the house and away from Blake and his super-powered pheromones. They are every bit as potent as my whacked out personal electromagnetic field, the one that shorts out the kitchen radio when I get too close to it as I'm making my coffee.

After shorting out one too many coffeemakers, I've resorted to the French press.

I'd take out all the electrical stuff in the house, except I love music. And air conditioning in the heat of summer, and hot food that I don't have to cook over an open flame, cave-girl style.

Blake saunters into the kitchen as I'm pulling on my work boots. His light brown hair is mussed and his eyes are sleepy and his shoulders are broad. The sight of his bare chest and those cords of muscle in his forearms makes my clitoris politely inquire as to why we made him sleep on the couch last night. But I tell her to hush and promise her a trip to the sex toy factory *very soon*.

"Hey, my little prickly-dickly-pear," he says with a lazy grin. "You're looking lovely this morning."

"Prickly-dickly-pear?"

"Ah-ah. That's one nice thing I've said about you. Now you have to say your five nice things about me so we can get this marriage off on the right foot."

"Blake."

"The walls have ears," he whispers with a wink that makes me want to curl up in a puddle at his feet and ask him if he could please wink at me like that a few more times.

I definitely didn't get enough sleep last night.

But he's right.

I owe him five nice things, because this is my mess that he's helping me out of.

"Can I do two now and three later?"

"As the lady wishes." He moves to the sink, lifts the French press with the old coffee in it, sniffs it, nods, then puts it on the counter like he's going to make a second cup with the used grounds.

I shake my head, quieting my inner coffee snob, because however he wants to wake up is his business. "You're very good at fixing toasters and you have a nice chin."

He arches a brow. "Nice chin?"

"Yep. Strong, but not too strong. Acceptably pointy with no chin butt or distracting dimples. Not on board with chin dimples, you never know what might get lost in a crevice like that." I prop my hands on my hips with a nod that announces the subject closed. "I have a lot to do today —including calling around for a good lawyer—so I need to—"

"Kiss your husband goodbye?" he suggests.

I purse my lips. "No thanks, Mr. Morning Breath. You obviously just woke up."

He chuckles as if we're not sworn enemies, like this is just a normal morning for him, and I get a glimpse of the Blake everyone else in town sees. The sweet, easy-going guy who's unoffended by the idea that his breath might stink, and not at all grouchy about sleeping on the couch or drinking old coffee at the start of his day.

"So I'll get my other three nice things over dinner?" he asks.

"Can't do dinner. It's bingo night. I volunteer. And everyone who plays is old, so it starts at dinnertime so they can all get home for bedtime at eight."

"You can't talk during bingo?"

"Not when they're calling numbers. It's against the—oh. You mean you want to come with me?"

"Naturally."

I laugh. "Ha. No."

He grins again. "If you said *yes*, I'd count that as one of your five nice things about me."

"*No.*" He can't come to bingo.

Tonight is *sexy* bingo, and while I'm perfectly comfortable with the fact that there's a sex toy factory in the middle of Happy Cat, and I can talk about dildos and cock rings and lube with the best of them, I *do not* want to discuss them around Blake.

Because then I'll start thinking even more about sex—specifically sex *with him*—and that's a complication I don't need in my life right now.

"Where you go, I go," he tells me. "That's what husbands and wives do."

"Except you have a job and I have a job and our jobs aren't together."

He lifts a shoulder. "Just taking delivery of a grape crusher today. You could come watch. Not every day you get to see that. What time's bingo?"

I pause, and is it just me, or is his smile getting sexier with every passing minute?

"Never mind. I'll ask Ryan. Pretty sure he goes with Cassie, doesn't he?"

I huff. "I have to—"

"Take care of the animals. Yep. Got it. You have a good day, my little cookie crumble."

I manage to escape the house without us touching, which is good, because easy-going morning Blake is like a magnet. My body wants to plaster itself against him even as my mind blares out warning sirens about getting in over my head.

Thankfully, I eventually lose myself in caring for, feeding, pasturing, and cleaning up after the dozens of animals on my ten acres, where I take in everything from horses, goats, and alpacas to dogs and cats to the occasional peacock, ferret, or hamster.

Chewpaca and Too-Pac are happy to see me, both humming low in their throats as they come over to the gate in their raised barn stall when I greet them. The horses across the way are also grateful for breakfast, and soon half my charges are out in the pastures, prancing and grazing and enjoying the early morning.

The baby goats go crazy for hanging out with Chewy again this morning, like they always do, and I get in a good round of fetch with the six dogs currently in my care, making sure to love on each and every one of them, because sometimes Buddy lets the other dogs push him to the back of the pack, and I don't want him to think I don't see him too.

It's hard work, but it's so worth it to know I'm giving all of these creatures a safe home with nothing to worry about.

The only hitch in the morning is the moment Blake comes out to say goodbye, planting a smacker on me for Dean's benefit.

He makes it last just long enough to offend the peacock and to make me want more, leaving me to stare at his back, filled with lusty thoughts as he walks away.

Damn. He gets to me. The knowledge that he's crashing bingo tonight and we have to put on a good show weighs heavier on me with every passing hour.

For his part, Dean doesn't try to hide, just sits there watching me all day long.

I pass him once not long after my morning volunteers have left. He's outside his car on a faded purple mat doing yoga stretches.

"Morning," he calls.

I wave, then feel guilty about it, remembering Blake's warning that Dean is *not* our friend.

Though he could be.

"It's afternoon," I call back.

"Not in Hawaii. I'm on Hawaii time. It's almost the same as being on regular time, except I get to pretend I'm on a beach." He grins. "You ever let people pay to ride your horses? I rode a horse once when I was a kid. It threw me off, but I got back on it, because that's what my parents said I needed to do. But it threw me off again, so I decided I should probably stick with riding bikes."

"Good decision," I reply. "I love horses, but they can be a skittish species."

"Where's your husband?" he asks.

"Um, I...don't think I'm supposed to tell you that," I say, sharing a friendly chuckle with the man who's spying on me. Nope. Not weird at all. "Where did Kyle find you?"

"Oh, me and him go way back," he says, clearly joking. "Actually I just met him a couple of weeks ago, while I was looking into something for someone else. You know. A confidential matter. But he seems like a good guy. I like him." He reaches for the back pocket of his workout shorts. "You want a card? In case you need any detective work done?"

I shake my head. "No, thank you, but you should pin one up on the board at the bakery on the square in town. People go there looking for all kinds of things."

I head inside for a short break and call Mr. Ashford, who confirms that Kyle may, indeed, be able to contest the validity of my marriage for the purposes of inheriting Gram's property. He also kindly suggests a few other lawyers who might be able to help me if we have to go to court.

I hang up to see that I've got a voicemail I missed while I was outside.

From a familiar number...

I lift the phone to my ear to hear my mother's voice. "Hope, I'm calling from Paris. I've heard some disturbing rumors about you getting *married* to one of those tacky O'Dells to satisfy some ridiculous clause in your grandmother's will. If this is true, it's disgraceful. Either way, call me as soon as possible. We need to head this off before it gets any worse."

The *only* ray of sunshine in my parents being offended by my marriage is that they're in Europe until August. They took off as soon as Gram was buried.

Hopefully, by the time they get back everything will have worked itself out and I can ask forgiveness for embarrassing them and we can all move on with our lives.

But seriously, thank god they're in Europe. It certainly wouldn't look good in court if my own mother is going around spreading rumors that I might be fake-married.

Downhearted, I put off calling her back and head outside to meet a farmer who needs to rehome a cow with stomach issues.

All I want is for Chewpaca to have a good life.

For *all* the animals to have a good life.

Why is Kyle so determined to wreck the good thing I've got going on the farm?

I'd wonder why my parents can't support me too, but I figured out a long time ago that we don't see eye-to-eye on anything, and that it's often the people who are supposed to love us the most who let us down the hardest.

By five, I haven't seen or heard from Blake. Dean has disappeared, which I assume means he's figured out where Blake is and is over spying on him now.

I begin to hope I'll get all the way to bingo without my other half, and won't have to worry about the tension and weirdness of pretending to be married in public.

I finish up my chores and head inside, but when I step out of my bathroom in a towel after a nice hot shower thirty minutes later, there's a man in my bedroom.

I stop myself mid-scream, because the man is my husband.

Technically.

He's in dirty jeans and work boots and is also in the middle of peeling his tee shirt over his head. There's a dirt smudge on his cheek and he has the same farmer tan that I do, which shouldn't be attractive, except it totally is when it's on those biceps I want to bite into like the last slice of triple chocolate cake.

"What are you doing?" I croak.

"Bingo time. Need to shower." He shucks his pants, and lord have mercy, love a duck and grant me strength, because Blake O'Dell in black boxer shorts should be cast in iron and put on display in the town square as a model of male perfection for women everywhere to admire.

Though they'll need to install a drinking fountain next to it to help with all the swooning.

"There's a shower down the hall in the guest bath," I force out around my dry tongue.

His gaze drifts to my towel, and his green eyes go dark. "I'm sure there is."

I inch toward the closet, which isn't large enough for me to hide in. "You just go on then... In there. While I do my... stuff out here."

"*Stuff*, hm?" He hums, his tongue slipping out to trace the seam of his lips. "So you want me to go into the shower and think about all the *stuff* you're doing all alone in here?"

"I'm getting dressed." My cheeks go hot, as I add in a hiss, "Not touching myself."

"Hey. No judgment here." He shrugs. "And you don't have to touch yourself. I could touch you instead. I mean, you're naked. I'm almost naked. Sex just seems a more mutually enjoyable option at this point, right?"

There's no edge to his words.

Correction: there's no *baiting* edge to his words.

But there are smoky edges and seductive edges and I have to concentrate very, *very* hard on remembering why sex with Blake is a bad idea.

Actually, I'm still struggling to pull up my list of Why Hopes Don't Bang Blakes when he brushes past me with a grin and heads into the bathroom. "All right, suit yourself. But don't leave without me, wifey-lifey. Or I'll have to come get you from bingo and spank you in public."

Two days ago, he couldn't say anything that didn't irritate the snot out of me.

Today, he can't say anything that doesn't rev my engines and then some. Gah, I have to get him out of here before it's too late. But I can't.

The alpaca.

I'm doing this for Chewy, because he's sweet and innocent and deserves a good life.

I throw on clothes as fast as I can and retreat to the living room, where I peek through the blinds and verify that yep, Dean's back.

He's setting up a telescope, which is a little weird, because the sun won't set for a few hours still, and if it was a telephoto lens designed to see all the way into the house, some part of it would have to actually be pointed *at* the house, which it's not.

Maybe Blake and I *can* pull this off.

Who knew Kyle would hire an inept private eye more interested in practicing yoga and star-gazing than hardcore spying?

"Ready, snugglepuff?" Blake leans in the doorway. He's always leaning. So casual. Not a care in the world. "We don't want to B-8 to bingo. Get it? B-8? Be late?"

"That is the worst joke ever," I tell him, but I'm smiling.

He frowns. "Hold on. You've got something..."

He reaches for my face. I assume he's going to wipe off dirt I missed in the shower. Instead, he goes in for the full-body kiss.

The one where his thighs line up with mine, our bellies press together, and his lips claim my mouth with an intensity that makes me want to stay inside and offer up my whole body to him on a platter. With side dishes. And garnish.

He kisses me, and I feel so...

So...

Worth it.

Worth a gorgeous man's time, attention, and complete focus.

I know I'm not his favorite person in the world, and he'll probably hate me even more before our fake marriage is over. But he still makes me feel like I'm doing something oh-so-right.

Like maybe it's okay that I'm a bit of a mess when it comes to feelings. I'm still a woman he'd love to spend more time with anyway.

Or possibly this is just lust, and we're both getting swept up in the heat.

He thrusts his fingers through my hair and angles the kiss deeper while I debate the merits of holding on to the last scraps of my resolve. What's so great about resolve, anyway? Isn't that just another way of saying you're too stubborn to change your mind?

I don't know. It's so hard to think clearly with his hands on me, his mouth on me. He smells like soap and sunshine, and he tastes like dessert, and I've pretty much decided I'm down for dessert for dinner and calling in sick to bingo night.

But before I can confess my weakness, he pulls away.

"There," he says in that smoky, sultry, sinful voice. "*Now* you look like a newlywed." He slaps me on the bottom, making me yip as he starts for the door. "Come on, cinnamon twist. The old folks are waiting."

TEN

Hope

I'm still replaying that kiss over and over again in my head when Blake parks his truck in front of the Happy Cat Community Center. Usually, bingo is at the senior center, but when Sunshine Toys announced they were sponsoring this week's prizes, the town's ladies went crazy reserving their spots, so bingo got moved to a bigger location.

We're not even out of the truck before the squealing starts.

"It's the newlyweds!"

"Oh, my, he must be *very* good in bed."

"*Shh!* If they want to have a quickie in the truck, let them."

"Mom, we're not having sex in public," Blake says to the last one.

Minnie O'Dell beams at him as she smothers me in a hug. "You should. Your father and I used to—"

"Ma, gross!"

"I know he's just saying that for my benefit." She giggles. "And welcome to the family, Hope. We're *so* glad it was you. And we'll have to plan a reception. Three of my boys, happily married. I'm so thrilled. *So* thrilled."

She links arms with both of us and leads us into the one-story building. My shoes squeak on the vinyl tile, but the noise is quickly drowned out by the gasps, and then the clapping.

Sorry, Blake mouths to me over his mom's head, not looking the least bit sorry.

The bird woman with the cupcakes from yesterday is sliding a sheet cake out of a box on a side table, muttering to herself, and there's a line of senior citizens waiting to buy paper bingo cards and dabbers.

"I need to go—" I start, but before I can finish with *check in for volunteer duty,* Ruthie May and her grand-daughter Emma June tackle us too.

"Hope! Blake! You came! Here. We saved you a spot at our table."

"We're not playing, we're working," I say.

Ruthie May clucks her tongue. "You're not volunteering on your wedding week! The luck is with you. Come. Sit. We already bought you cards."

"We got it covered, Hope," Ryan calls. Blake's oldest brother is a fireman by day, but tonight he's in a bingo apron with dabbers tucked into one pocket and a sample of the evening's prizes tucked into another. "You sit and play." He pulls out a giant purple dildo. "If you're lucky, maybe you'll take this puppy home. Since I know what else you're sleeping with."

He winks, and Blake tosses a dabber at him. "Very funny, old man."

Three of the regular elderlies in sun visors, Palm Springs shirts, and matching pastel pants descend on us. "It's your turn to play," Greta says.

"I have a lucky feeling about you tonight," Eunice adds.

"That's just gas," Phoebe tells Eunice. "But Olivia did my star chart today, and she said I'd lose to newlyweds, so I'll let you pretend your gas is a lucky feeling. But if you win that vibrator, you have to promise to give it to me."

There's a groan from the cake table, and the pixie woman kicks one of the legs. I still haven't met her, and I need to fix that, but she doesn't look like she's having the best day, and Olivia's gliding over to help.

"Just *had* to crack, didn't you?" the bakery lady says to the cake.

"That's a hell of a break." Dean slides next to her and aims his camera down at it. "Bad omen for those newly-weds, you ask me. I'm Dean. You know those two?"

She turns and throws her hands up in Cassie's direction. "I tried, I really did. I'm so sorry. But it should still taste great, and I'll refund your money as soon as I get back to my computer. Cracked cakes are on the house!"

Without answering Dean, she slips out of the room.

"You know these two?" Dean turns the question to Cassie, who's wearing a sling that matches Olivia's, though hers is filled with hedgehogs, not baby. Olivia must have decided Princess and Duchess deserved a night out.

Both the hedgehogs squeak indignantly at Dean's question and Cassie shoots him a *get lost* look.

Princess and Duchess are possibly the most adorable hedgehogs I've ever seen, and they won the owner lottery when they got Olivia. They're hugely popular at bingo night—all the senior citizens love cooing over them almost as much as they love fussing over Clover Dawn, now that she's here. Poor Olivia seemed to be pregnant forever.

Not that she complained.

She seemed to love every minute of it, but then, Olivia would find something to love about having to live in an igloo outside an extra stinky paper factory.

Greta glares at Dean and shoves me into a chair. "Nosy old badger."

"Trying to take over my role," Ruthie May adds with a sniff.

"Grandma." Emma June smothers her in a hug. "You know that's never going to happen."

Blake sucks in a deep breath as he plops into the chair next to me and swings an arm around my shoulders. "Nothing like bingo night in Happy Cat. You smell that? That's the smell of determination, rivalry, markers, and Ben-Gay."

I shift a look at him, and I can't help myself.

I crack up laughing.

He grins.

And *this* is what acting like a happily married couple must look like.

Odd.

It *feels* so normal.

And happy.

"Did you see?" Eunice asks. "We got you all a wedding cake. We didn't know if you'd be here, or if you'd be home doing the horizontal mamba, but we would've eaten the cake with or without you. Who doesn't love cake?"

"I love cake," Blake says. Dean angles closer to us, and my fake hubby adds, "Almost as much as I love Hope and all her animals."

"People! Places! Numbers are about to start!" Cassie calls.

There's a mad rush for seats. An old guy tackles Ryan to get to the last dabber, and someone calls someone else a shit-head who's going down.

"See this?" Blake leans closer, giving me a whiff of his clean scent and another opportunity to ogle his sexy hand as he sets it over my bingo cards. "This is our future, baby. I can't wait."

"Take your time, young whippersnapper," Phoebe tells him. "Have a few dozen babies first."

"We already have baby goats," I tell her.

"Hmm. Good start, but there's nothing like projectile baby poo at three AM to solidify a marriage."

"We're still practicing," Blake says with a wink.

All three of the sun visor brigade fan themselves.

"I would be too if I was hitched up to you," Eunice says.

"Mm-hmm," the other two agree.

"That's my son you're talking to. In front of his wife," Minnie O'Dell warns from the next table over.

"You think Tucker will ever propose?" Emma June asks Ruthie May with a sigh.

"Honey, I know what you see in that boy, but the smarts to buy a ring ain't it."

"We're starting with the green cards," Cassie yells, and the room falls silent as we all bend over our cards.

"Holy shit, we have like eight of these," Blake mutters.

"Each," I agree. "You don't go to Happy Cat bingo and not play the hell out of Happy Cat bingo."

"Usually I do sixteen on my own," Greta says with a pout, "but they wouldn't let me on account of there being so many people here tonight."

"So you two haven't ever played bingo together before?" Dean asks. "Interesting."

"We haven't gone bungee jumping or cow tipping together either, in case you're taking notes," Blake replies. "That's next week."

I almost poke him, but we're playing happy newlyweds. "I can't wait, honey-bear."

"B-Four!" Cassie calls with the help of the snuffling hedgehogs.

"And after!" the whole room choruses back.

I should be up walking around with Ryan, Jace, and Olivia—and the baby, of course—making sure no one's dabbers are out of ink or diving in with a towel if someone spills a drink on the cards or chasing George Cooney off the cake table, since the trash panda has just climbed up on top of it and looks ready to dive in.

George is a common sight around town, but I've never seen him at bingo before.

"Did Ryan mention if George Cooney was feeling better today?" I ask Blake as Ryan scoops the massive animal off the cake table and carries him to the door.

George chitters.

"Hush, you overgrown trash panda. We don't eat other people's wedding cake," Ryan chides.

"Just said he had the burps," Blake replies. "Why?"

"Cassie said he had too much peanut butter yesterday. We were worried."

"Ah. Pretty sure he survived."

"Shh!" the sun visor brigade hisses at us.

"G-Forty-seven!" Cassie says.

We manage to lose on the green cards, the red cards, the yellow cards, and the purple cards. Gordon wins a Sunshine Toys starter pack with a dildo, a vibrator, anal beads, and lube in it. Eunice wins a toy of the month subscription. Mrs. O'Dell wins the lube sample pack and a gift certificate to a lingerie store in Atlanta.

And while I'm sitting there with friends, playing bingo to win sex toys, I start to relax and slip into a new pattern with Blake.

He reaches over to mark an O-Sixty-nine that I missed. I press my red dabber to his nose, and soon we're both laughing and acting like teenagers as he tries to pay me back.

But that's not his end goal.

Oh, no.

The man fakes me out with the dabber and gets me with a sneak kiss attack while someone across the room yells out a loud *Bingo!*

"Hmm," Dean mutters from the table behind us. "This is gonna be harder than Kyle said it would be."

We're doing it!

We're selling our marriage.

That, as much as anything, puts a real smile on my face.

"Blue cards, people! Grand prize time," Cassie calls.

Ryan struts to the front of the room and walks the purple dildo around, Vanna White-style.

"Somebody's going home *really* lucky tonight," Ruthie May says. "That's our most popular vibrating dildo. It can really work out some kinks, if you know what I mean."

"It's totally my favorite," Emma June agrees.

"I tried it once and it overheated my cooch," Phoebe says. She's the smallest of the bunch—no more than five feet tall, and maybe ninety-five pounds—with smile lines creasing her elfin face.

Ruthie May gasps. "Uh, it's not supposed to do that. Do

you still have it? Our lab technicians might need to take a look."

"Wasn't the dildo's fault. I was storing it over my oven. I spent all day Thanksgiving baking. By the time everyone finally left, I was ready to de-stress. But the oven was still on, so that sucker was about a hundred and forty degrees when I stuck it up the ol' biscuit basket."

Now we *all* gasp.

And she grins. "Just kidding. Not a dildo girl, never have been. They aren't up to handling all this sexiness."

"I-Seventeen," Cassie calls, and we all breathe a sigh of relief and turn our focus back to our bingo cards.

Blake absently rubs his thumb over my arm just below my shirt sleeve, and I'm not actually certain it's absently. Because he has a gleam in his eyes, and he hasn't asked me to say three more nice things about him, though I know he hasn't forgotten.

He wouldn't forget.

Blake remembers everything, which is one of the things I really like about him, though I'm not quite ready to confess that just yet.

"You hold that dabber expertly," I say to him instead, holding up three fingers.

"Mrs. O'Dell, you surprise me," he murmurs.

I reach down and squeeze his solid thigh, because it's there, and we're supposed to be playing the happily married couple, and I *do* like touching him.

I can touch him here.

In public.

It's not nearly as dangerous as touching him in private.

Also, this last game is taking *forever*.

Since this is the grand prize, we have to fill our *entire* card instead of just getting a single row.

Which means I have all the time in the world to lean closer. Let myself indulge in the fantasy that we actually *could* be the couple playing bingo in matching shirts with Blake's brothers and their wives while talking about which sex toys are new at the factory.

I sigh dreamily just as Blake shouts, "Bingo!"

"A big purple dildo to the newlyweds!" Cassie cries. "Get up here, you crazy kids, and show off what you just won!"

"If the newlyweds need a dildo, they're doing something wrong," Carl yells.

"If you don't need a dildo, what are you doing here?" Greta yells back.

Blake and I stare at each other, and a moment later, we're both laughing so hard my eyes are tearing up.

A dildo. And not just any dildo.

We're the newlyweds who won the dildo to end all dildos.

It's like they *knew* I needed something to take the edge off of not sleeping with Blake, even though everyone is laughing and ribbing us and treating this like one big ol' bachelorette party.

"Maybe if you're lucky, she'll show you how she uses it," Ryan says with a wink when we make our way to the front of the room to claim Blake's prize.

"And now cake!" Cassie cries, fighting through the crowd with the hedgehogs in a sling, to congratulate us. "Cake first, and *then* fun times with the dildo."

"In private," Olivia adds as she and Jace and the baby also arrive in the midst of the crowd. "Apparently there are laws about public nudity. Silly laws. But still laws."

She smiles at me, and I hug her tight, then pull Cassie in as well.

I might not know much about marriage, but these women have taught me everything I know about family and community.

I glance over their shoulders to see Blake watching me with a soft expression that makes my heart ache in the good way. Maybe, just maybe, he has some things to teach me too.

ELEVEN

Blake

We laugh the entire way home, in complete agreement that the entire town was in cahoots to make sure we took home the purple dildo. We both saw at least one other full card on our way up to claim our prize.

And maybe it was our cracked but delicious cake, or seeing George Cooney perched on the trash can looking very put-out for being denied sweets, or sitting with the sun visor brigade, but anytime one of us stops laughing, the other one snorts, and we both start rolling all over again.

It's a wonder we make it home safely without Hope's energy field shorting out my truck. But the hula man on the dash seems extra happy and bouncy, swinging his hips and strumming his ukulele in time with our laughter.

Our shadow follows us through the dusky evening light, parking in his spot across the road—apparently Dean the overly friendly private eye is going to be camping in the

Frick's field for the next month—but the fact that we're being watched isn't why I hurry around the truck to open Hope's door.

It's because Operation: Real Romance is in full effect, and damn if it doesn't seem to be working.

I certainly haven't seen her smile like that in...

Huh. I can't remember.

Not the last time she smiled at *me* like that, anyway.

"You want to take this inside?" she asks, holding out our hard-won bingo treasure with a giggle. "I need to go check on the fur babies. Rick, my part-time hand, feeds and stables them on Bingo Night, but I like to do a stable check to make sure everyone's okay."

"I'll come with you." I tuck the dildo down the front of my pants, letting the massive purple head peek up near my right hip, making Hope giggle again.

"That's obscene."

"No, it's not." I stroke the dildo protectively. "Don't talk that way about Dildo Shaggins."

"Dildo Shaggins? Oh my god." Her head falls back as she braces an arm on my shoulder and laughs so hard she clearly has to struggle to stay upright.

I want to make her laugh like that every day.

At least once a day.

"But I can't take credit for the name," I admit. "It's from *Fellowship of the G-Strings*, a hobbit soft porn spin-off."

She laughs harder. "Hobbit porn. What in the world? Why are people so weird?"

"Says the woman who's willing to do whatever it takes to protect an innocent alpaca and his sperm."

"Well, alpaca sperm. That's a totally different thing." She sobers abruptly, but I can see the grin still teasing at her lips. "A very serious thing."

"Very serious," I echo. "We should go check on him and make sure no one has run away with his balls."

She laughs as she leads the way toward the stable. "If people had any idea how valuable he is, I'd probably have to hire security."

I cut a glance her way, but I can't get a read on her expression in the dim light of the solar lights along the path. "Well, Kyle knows."

"But Kyle is family. He's a rat, but a relatively honorable rat. He'd never outright steal, especially when it would be easy for people who know what they're doing to trace him. It's not like the alpaca sperm black market is huge, you know? No, he'll do it the legal way. The St. Claire way. In court." She sighs, but it's a relaxed sound, not a stressed out one. "But looks like that's not going to be a problem. Fingers crossed and knock on wood, but I think we brought the romance tonight. If I didn't know better, I'd never believe we were about to kill each other just last night."

I grunt. "We weren't going to kill each other. It was just a fight."

"I told you I hated you."

"Well, I can bring out the worst in people," I say, stepping to the side as she opens the padlock on the barn door and slides it to the right, even though I'm pretty sure she's the only person I bring out the worst in. But if I'm going to win her over, I have to shoulder some of the blame too. "Too stubborn for my own good. And I'm always right so that can be hard to handle at times, I'm sure."

She snort-laughs. "Oh, please. What have you been right about lately? Today for example?"

"I was mostly kidding," I say as I follow her inside. "But I was right about going to bingo with you. Brilliant idea, that one."

She hums beneath her breath as she climbs up on the top rung of the wooden gate on our left. "True. We put on a good show. And it *was* fun."

I catch the back of her tee shirt as she leans over to check on the pen of mama goats, most of which are already asleep. She glances over her shoulder, casting my hand an amused look.

"Just making sure you don't fall in," I say.

She arches a brow. "I do this every night. Haven't fallen in yet."

"There's always a first time."

"If I did take a tumble, the worst that could possibly befall me is a good licking from worried mama goats." She smiles. "But I appreciate the concern."

"My pleasure," I say, reluctantly releasing my grip on her tee as she climbs down and starts across the barn, scanning the other pens as we go. "So you have to pen the males separate from the females and the babies?"

"Yeah. I separate the mamas and babies at night so I can get milk from the mamas in the morning. The bucks are separate from everyone else and the other bucks or they get aggressive with each other. I do my best to make sure each buck has a fixed male friend to sleep with overnight, though. Goats are social creatures and get lonely, but I'm trying to keep the herd a manageable size so I can't just pen them together and let 'em go at it." She sighs. "Though honestly, sometimes keeping the bucks away from the ladies feels like my full-time job."

"Randy suckers, huh?"

She rolls her eyes. "So randy. Zeus has devoured three fences in the past year. He's *that* determined to get to whichever doe is currently in heat. He's horrified more than one group of school kids trying to mount the ladies."

She jabs a thumb over her shoulder. "Half the babies are his."

"Shouldn't have named him Zeus. Clearly gave him a god complex. Next boy goat gets named Brian. Or Greg."

She grins. "Kevin."

"Nigel."

"Yes, Nigel, that's perfect," she says with a laugh. "Next batch of boy babies, they'll all be Nigel. I'm sure that will solve the randy problem in no time."

Doubtful. My name could be Nigel Periwinkle Manboobington the 3rd, and I'd still chew through a fence to get to Hope. I'm that desperate to touch her, a fact I'm sure is going to make getting to sleep tonight as hellish as it was last night.

But at least tonight, she'll head to bed without hating me.

It's a small victory, but definitely a start in the right direction.

She stops beside the last stall and looks in on the animals. "But these boys don't need to be Nigels. They're as sweet as they come, and the baby goats adore them. The kids follow Chewy everywhere. I can't hardly keep them apart. Probably because they know he watches over them, keeping the predators scared away."

Two fluffy alpacas are snoozing snuggled together in the hay on the far side of the pen. "You know Chewpaca, of course." She points to the larger animal on the right before shifting her finger to the left. "And that's Too-Pac, his new best buddy."

"Nice. So alpaca boys don't fight?"

"Oh, they can, but luckily these two get along really well. And alpacas can actually die of loneliness, so it's important that Chewpaca has a friend. Too-Pac is a little younger and naturally submissive, so I'm sure that helps." She glances up at me, a mischievous smile on her face. "Once the pecking order has been established, animals almost always calm down and get along. People too, I've found."

I return her grin. "Is that right?"

"Yes." She turns, leaning back against the gate as she lifts her chin. "So I expect we'll be fine from here on out."

"Yeah?" I brace a hand on the wood beside her head. "Now that you've come to terms with the fact that I'm your alpha alpaca?"

She laughs softly, her grin spreading to take up her entire face, sending a surge of awareness rushing through me. "Oh, please. It's clear that *I'm* the alpha alpaca. I have a much fluffier, more glorious pelt." She pats my chest through my tee shirt, her fingers warm despite the cool spring night. "But that's okay. I like beta males."

I try to stop smiling and put on a faux angry face, but my lips refuse to cooperate. "I am not your beta, woman. I'm an untamed man-beast who eats rocks for breakfast and spits nails for lunch."

"Because that makes sense."

"Go on. Say it. *You're my alpha alpaca, Blake.* That'll be your fourth nice thing about me today."

She laughs again, her fingertips trailing down my chest nearly to my belt buckle before she pulls her hand away, making me fifty percent harder with that one simple touch. Pretty soon I'll be giving Dildo Shaggins a run for his money.

Maybe I should have taken him inside, after all. Made more room in my pants.

"Personally," she says, "I prefer a man who's okay with his woman taking the lead."

His woman. Just hearing her say those two words together makes me want her even more. Want her to be mine. *My* woman.

My Hope and my hope.

Capital and lowercase.

She makes me feel things I haven't felt in so long, dare to wish for something more than a workaholic life spent chasing professional success so hard I barely have the energy to shower by the time I'm finished for the day, let alone go looking for love.

But that's because I haven't wanted love, not really.

I already found it four years ago, and some stubborn part of my heart refuses to let go of that dream, the one that ends with Hope and me waking up in the same bed every morning for the rest of our lives.

Just because *she* wasn't ready four years ago doesn't mean *I* wasn't. We were great friends growing up and all it took was one night, seeing her in a different light, for me to want so much more. To want it all.

I bring my free hand to the other side of her head, trapping her between my arms while I lean closer, smile falling away as I whisper, "So where would you lead me, Miss Alpha? If I handed you my reins?"

Her tongue slips out to tease across her lips as her gaze drops to my mouth, leaving little doubt that she wants to be kissed as badly as I want to kiss her.

"Nowhere in particular," she murmurs. "At least not right now. Just like to know I've got the option."

"Liar," I counter. "I think you know exactly where you want to go. And what you want me to do to you when we get there."

Her chest rises and falls faster. "Blake," she whispers,

my name a warning and a confession and a plea for mercy all wrapped up in one.

I tip my forehead closer to hers. "Just tell me what you want. Because I promise, whatever it is, I want to give it to you. I like making you happy a hell of a lot more than making you hate me."

"I've never hated you." Her breath rushes out, caressing my lips, turning a wheel inside of me another crank, until the tension is almost unbearable. "I've never hated you. I'm sorry. I shouldn't have said that. Of all people, I should know better. But—never mind. I just want..."

"Yes?" I prompt after the silence stretches on for a beat. I want to ask why she should know better, but I get the feeling that's not where I should press right now.

She'll tell me when she's ready.

"I mean, I *don't* want..." Her head tips back and her nose brushes against mine.

She moans softly, a sound that echoes through me, making me ache to kiss her, crush her body to mine, show her right here on the floor of the barn how much I want to give her pleasure.

But I've fallen into this trap before.

I'm not going to push. I'm going to wait until Hope asks for it, begs for it. I want her to own this decision, to own how much she wants me too, for once in our fraught personal history.

"Tell me, Mrs. O'Dell," I say, my lips so close to hers that her body heat warms my skin. "I want to know what you want and don't want and everything in between."

She sucks in a breath and ducks under my arm. "I can't do this."

I spin to face her. "Why not?"

"I just can't," she says, her cheeks pink and her gaze

looking everywhere but at me. "I can't keep making the same mistakes. People don't change, no matter how much you might want them to."

"I disagree," I say, but she's already rushing on.

"And it's not fair to ask them to. Not when what they want is a perfectly fine thing to want. I mean, asking Kyle to quit making fun of me for dropping out of vet school is one thing. Or asking my parents to stop using me as a go-between." She takes a step back, shaking her head faster. "But fair or not, no one ever changes. They say they will, and then they go right back to business as usual, like all the crying and begging and bargaining never happened in the first place. I just can't do it. I can't try to change knowing I'm doomed to fail, and so there's no point in even trying."

My brow furrows. "I won't make you cry, Hope. And you'll never have to beg me for anything. Not ever."

Her throat works and her eyes begin to shine, but she still won't look at me. "You've already made me cry. I just never let you know about it."

Her words break my damned heart. I've been so focused on my own pain over being rejected that I've completely overlooked hers. I've been a fucking asshole, and I'm ready to admit it. I'm ready to confess and ask for forgiveness and beg for a second chance if that's what it takes.

But before I can say a word, Hope exhales sharply and points a finger over my shoulder. "Oh, watch out."

I start to turn, but there's already a long, silky neck wrapped around mine, pinning me gently, but insistently, to the gate. "Hey, Chewpaca," I grunt out, reaching up to scratch his ears. "Good to see you too, buddy. How'd you get all the way up here?"

"His stall—it's on a platform," she says softly. "Helps me keep the straw dry for them."

He lets out a musical hum-purr that vibrates through my chest, easing a little of the misery there.

I get both hands involved with the scratching. "Yeah, you're a good boy. We've got to keep you here with your mama. You'd miss her, wouldn't you? She's pretty much the best."

Hope watches me with soft eyes as she strokes Chewpaca's nose. "I am not the best, but I try to be a good person. Try really hard." She smiles a sad smile. "And that's why I can't make you promises I can't keep. And I won't. Because you're a good person too. And I really want you to be happy."

She leans in, kissing Chewpaca's cheek before patting him on the neck. "Good night, Chewy." She steps back, blowing me a kiss. "Good night, Blake. I'll see you in the morning."

"In the morning," I echo, taking up Chewy petting duties as I watch her go. I wait until she's out of the barn before I whisper to the alpaca, "I'm getting the feeling she thinks there's no middle ground for us, friend."

Chewpaca hums again, but lower in his throat this time.

"Exactly," I agree. "There's always middle ground if you're willing to look hard enough. And if you don't give up."

The alpaca shakes his head, tossing the long silk on his neck.

"Don't worry, buddy, I won't," I promise. "I'm not ready to give up on your mama. Not even close."

With one last ear scratch, I wish Chewy a good night and head for the house, where I set Dildo Shaggins in a position of honor by the French press—hoping it will make Hope laugh in the morning—and get ready for bed.

I toss and turn on the couch for a solid hour, but finally

exhaustion wins out and I fall into a restless sleep, only to be awakened at two AM by a shuffling silhouette shambling through the darkness like something straight out of a zombie flick.

It's Hope, I realize as my brain casts off the sleep fog.

Of course it is.

Who else would be wandering around her house in the middle of the night?

But her arms hang loose at her sides and her head is cocked at an unnatural angle and I'm pretty sure she's...

"Hope? Are you awake?" I ask softly, my voice a gentle rumble in the dark.

"Mmm," she hums before drawling, "corn chips sippy cup."

I grin. "What was that?"

"For the baby elephant," she says, her words slurred.

"Of course," I say, cursing myself for plugging my phone in to charge in the kitchen. I'd never show it to anyone but her, but a video of this would make my entire year. "And where is the baby elephant now?"

"Under the covers," she mumbles. "He's hiding."

"Why's he hiding?"

"Scared of the chickens. Gonna get him corn chips in a sippy cup. Make him feel better." She sighs and her head lolls heavily to the other side. "But I'm soooo sleepy."

I draw back the sheet and quilt covering my legs. "Then crawl in and take a rest. The couch is big enough for two and I'm sure the baby elephant will be fine. The chickens went to bed too."

"Oh, good." She shuffles forward and sit-falls onto the cushion beside me. "So tired. Couldn't fall asleep. Too worried."

"What were you worried about, baby?" I ask, tucking

the blanket chastely between us. I would never take advantage, but I don't feel bad about having her here beside me. She's safer tucked against me than sleep-wandering around the house banging into furniture in the dark.

"Blake," she sighs, turning onto her side and snuggling closer to my chest. "I just want to kiss him sooooo much."

My heart flips. "I'm pretty sure he feels the same way." I hesitate, guilt warring with the need to put in a good word for myself while she's in a receptive state of mind. Finally I add, "And kissing could be fun. Worth a try, I think. You should definitely kiss Blake tomorrow."

"No," she mutters, her body going heavy against mine as she seems to sink into a deeper level of sleep. "No kissing. Don't get to have fun. No fun for Hope. All alone. Just alone. And safe. And sad. Hugging the baby elephant."

I wrap an arm around her and kiss her forehead, falling a little more in love with her with every passing minute. That's what this is, what it's always been for me. I'm in love with this woman, who's been in so much more pain than I ever realized.

But not anymore. No more alone. No more sad.

I'm going to show her that she can be safe in someone's arms too.

Mine.

TWELVE

Hope

I wake up delicious.

I am a sticky bun with extra icing.

I am a hot fudge sundae with bonus caramel sauce.

I am a two-hour massage followed by a sauna and a hot tub soak and finished off with a nap in a sea-side hammock.

I am boneless with delight, perfectly warm and perfectly cozy and perfectly held.

Held...

My brow furrows, but I keep my eyes closed as I drift more fully into wakefulness and do a full body scan.

Yes, that is indeed a big, strong arm wrapped around my ribs and nestled familiarly between my breasts. That is someone's sleepy breath stirring the hair on the top of my head and someone's long, lean, muscled form tucked against my back in the big spoon position. And that is most definitely someone's morning whack of dawn pressed against the base of my spine.

Despite all the years separating my first and latest experience with this particular sausage sunrise, I'd know it anywhere, even if Blake didn't happen to be the only man presently sleeping in my house. His cock has personality and a...*ahem*...girthiness that is unparalleled in the rest of my experience.

I squeeze my eyes even more tightly shut, mouthing a silent curse.

Damn sleepwalking, damn my weak sense of self-preservation, and damn Blake for letting me crawl in with him when I'm guessing it was pretty clear I was *not* operating consciously.

Damn him for feeling so damned good.

For holding me so damned perfectly.

And for possessing such damned fabulous slumber lumber.

I fully intend to read him the riot act—and set forth some very firm ground rules about how to handle a sleepwalking incident should it happen again—but first to escape with as much of my dignity intact as possible.

Moving stealthy like a ninja, I circle my fingers as far as I can around his wrist and lift the dead weight of his arm just high enough to give me room to slip under. I wiggle forward, centimeter by torturous centimeter, but I'm still several inches from the edge of the couch when a husky voice murmurs, "Leaving so soon?"

I curse beneath my breath and release his arm like it's made of molten lava. He moves his hand to my hip, squeezing it through the covers with a familiarity that feels lovely.

Unfortunately, wondering what the hell I said to him

last night while I was sleep drunk feels equally shitty.

I hate not being in control like that. Especially when it puts me at someone else's mercy.

"Nothing happened," he says. "I just offered you a safe place to lie down with the covers between us. I was worried you might hurt yourself if I let you head off on your own."

My irritation evaporates in the warmth of his sweetly-intentioned words, but I'm still mortified, and will continue to be so until I know—"How bad was I? Did I say anything I need to apologize for?"

"No, not at all," he says, squeezing my hip again. "You didn't say much, actually. Just that you were really sleepy." He hesitates for a second before adding with laughter in his voice, "And something about getting some corn chips for a baby elephant in a sippy cup."

"Oh, god," I huff. Still, it could have been so much worse. I glance over my shoulder at him. "Sorry about that. I should have warned you about the sleepwalking. I was hoping it wouldn't be an issue."

"No big deal. Just worried me a little. You ever end up outside the house when you do that?"

"A couple of times," I confess, earning myself a disapproving rumble. "But not in a long time. Not since I put the extra locks on the door. My sleepwalking self seems to be too lazy to get through more than one or two before she gives up. And I don't do it all the time. Only when I'm super tired or...stressed."

"Sorry about that," he says softly.

"It's not your fault. It's Kyle and the detective and all the rest of it. And it could've been worse. Once I woke up and I'd shorted out the pencil sharpener and a spare TV that I kept in my office." I sigh. "Speaking of the rest of it, I should probably take Dean a cup of coffee."

"You should absolutely *not* take Dean a cup of coffee."

"It got chilly last night," I argue. "I'm sure he'd appreciate something hot to drink."

"And the chance to probe you for information while you're sleepy and your guard is down." He pats my ass. "You're too trusting."

"And you're patting my ass."

"It's a nice ass," he says. "And it's right there..."

"You're saying I should get up if I don't want my ass patted?"

"I'm saying you should stay right here," he says, wrapping his arm around my waist again. "And go back to sleep with me. It's barely six AM."

"I usually have the goats milked by seven-thirty and out in the pasture no later than eight." But my traitorous body is already relaxing against him.

He just feels so good. So right.

But he isn't right for you, and you're not right for him, and if you stay for snuggles you'll definitely be giving him the wrong impression. So get up, weakling. Loser. Beta alpaca. Fork in the spoon sandwich. You're lazier than George Cooney waiting on the couch for Cassie to hand him the popcorn bowl when it is literally five inches from his greedy little paw.

Finally the nagging voice in my head gets to be too much and I swing my legs to the floor with a sigh. "I really should get to the barn. I forgot I have to bottle feed a few of the babies today so they'll be ready to come with me to goat yoga in the square."

"Goat yoga?" Blake arches a brow and his lips curve up on one side, drawing my attention to his sexy morning stubble.

Damn, the man looks good with a little scruff.

And a tight white undershirt hugging his muscled biceps.

And a sexy case of bed head.

I drag my gaze away from him as I rake a hand through my own crazy hair, which I'm sure looks much less deliciously rumpled. "Yeah. Goat yoga. The babies climb over everyone while they're doing the poses. Star, the new yoga teacher, says it's a big thing these days. We had twenty-five people sign up for the demo class today. If all goes well, we'll probably start doing it once a week through the spring and summer."

"You need help getting them fed and loaded?" He sits up, but keeps the covers puddled around his waist, making me think a certain something hasn't calmed down yet. Which makes me start thinking about how perfect that certain something is, and how I've never come as hard or often as I did on our first wedding night, the one we both denied ever happened so we could get an annulment.

But it did happen.

And I've spent the past four years replaying highlights from that night in my head when I'm alone in the dark. Even though I know I shouldn't.

But nothing else gets me there. Even the few times I've slept with other men, sometimes I've found my thoughts drifting...

Shameless hussy, the inner voice pipes up, but her voice is softer now, so quiet it would be easy to ignore.

Which means it's time to get away from Blake. ASAP.

"Thanks, but I've got it," I say, heading for the bedroom. "I'm used to doing it all on my own."

"Doesn't mean it wouldn't be easier with two," he calls after me. "Maybe even more fun."

Oh, it would absolutely be more fun. But the "it" I'm

thinking about has nothing to do with milking goats or feeding animals.

If only it hadn't been so long since I'd been with someone. If only Blake's touch didn't set me on fire. If only this house were five times bigger so I could put some distance between us, and wouldn't end up bumping hips with him every day as we move about my tiny kitchen. Because even *that* is enough to make my knees weak and my willpower start to lose its grip on the edge of the cliff.

"You take cream, right?" Blake is standing by the fridge when I breeze into the kitchen after getting dressed in yoga pants and a tank top and jacket combo that will take me from the cool morning into the warm spring afternoon.

He's wearing a pair of brown Carhartt work pants that seriously do it for me, and that same white undershirt that's going to be starring in my fantasies later on. The nutty smell of coffee fills the air and what looks like a breakfast sandwich is wrapped in foil and sitting beside my cell phone, which is beside the French press, which is beside—

"Aaah!"

He glances at Dildo Shaggins and grins. "Oh. Sorry. Forgot he was there. You want me to move him?"

"No." I start to laugh, remembering bingo last night. "I like him. He's...happy."

Blake snort-laughs. "Clearly. He must like his new home."

"Or he thinks he's getting breakfast too."

"Never feed your dildo before midnight. It's a rule."

He lifts the cream.

I nod, and he adds a dollop to a to-go mug while I giggle at the cheesy eighties movie reference.

"Thank you." I tap the warm, foil-wrapped treat on the counter. "For me?"

"Yeah, egg and cheese on a toasted bagel. That good?"

"That's lovely. Thank you so much."

"Of course," he says, grinning. "I owe you for meatloaf night. Figured I could cook supper later too. If you don't mind something meaty on the grill or veggie pasta. That's about the extent of my culinary repertoire."

"That's a perfect repertoire. I'll pick up something from the butcher shop on my way home from yoga."

"Sweet." He holds out the to-go mug. "I'll be back around four or five. I've got to grab a few more things from my place and then do some work in the vineyard."

"Okay." I take the mug, feeling strangely torn.

"It's just supper, Hope," Blake says, reading me better than I'm reading myself. "Nothing to stress out about. There's no reason we shouldn't be good to each other, right?"

Oh, I want to be good to him, I want it more than I've wanted anything in longer than I can remember, but unfortunately my libido's idea of "good" and what's best for Blake aren't anywhere close to the same page.

They're not even in the same book.

So I force a smile and say, "Of course not. Friends should be good to each other. And I'm glad we're becoming real friends again. Truly. I need all the friends I can get."

He winks. "Think you can squeeze the word 'friends' in there one more time?"

I laugh beneath my breath. "Later, friend," I say, heading for the door.

"I'll be here," he replies.

Like I can count on him.

I'm starting to think this is real. That I really *can* count on him. Maybe for more than being a fake husband.

And isn't that a scary thought?

THIRTEEN

Blake

I linger inside just long enough to finish my coffee and put our few dishes in the sink. If I were at my place, I'd put them off until I had to do them, but I don't want to leave a mess for Hope.

Not when she keeps everything else so tidy.

I want to be a help, not a hindrance.

Dean is still watching us—seriously, does the dude never sleep?

Not that I mind right now, because it gives me an excuse to go find Hope before I leave.

There are a half dozen dogs dashing around the pasture amidst a few extremely plush-looking sheep, who don't seem fazed at all by the activity. A cat is perched on a fence-post, licking its hindquarters, and Chewpaca and Too-Pac are both grazing in the next fenced-in pasture over, standing guard over about a dozen frolicking baby goats.

Hope's still in the barn, finishing up the milking. "Hey, pretty pumpkin-poo," I call.

She uses her forearm to push hair back out of her face and laughs, which feels like a home run.

"So pretty pumpkin-poo is on the keeper list?" I ask.

She grins wider. "Nah. But the nicknames in general are starting to grow on me, monkey buns. Did you forget something?"

"Just to kiss my wife goodbye." I smile at her, and add in a softer voice, "In case someone's watching, of course."

Her eyes go momentarily wide, and then she gives the mama goat a quick pat. I feel a surge of guilt when I remember fighting with her *right here*, over the goat milking station, barely a year ago.

"Lucky me," she says, but the words are more breathless than sarcastic, and I high-five myself for finally doing the right thing here.

I smile at her. "And then you won't have to worry about so much as *looking* at me for hours and hours," I promise as we meet halfway between the milking station and the barn door.

"Looking at you isn't exactly a hardship," she confesses in a whisper.

"Don't spare my ego. I know you'd rather look at Dildo Shaggins."

She smiles, and I couldn't resist kissing her if my life depended on it.

So even though this is technically for the cameras and the detective and the sake of her alpaca, I enjoy every moment of my mouth capturing hers.

The way she threads her fingers through my hair.

The feel of her curves under those tight pants.

The taste of coffee on her lips.

The tickle of her breath on my skin.

A man could drown in a kiss like this.

Happily.

"Wow," she murmurs against my lips.

"Not bad, eh?"

"Passable." She giggles again while I chuckle. I consider going in for just one more, but she pokes me in the chest. Though, when she speaks, she still sounds as dazed as I feel. "Go on. Get out of here and get your work done."

Or neither of us will be getting any work done, I silently add.

I want to toss her over my shoulder and carry her back to her house and not get anything but *her* done today, but we both have commitments, and more importantly, I'm not going to rush this.

She's worth waiting for.

And I want her one hundred percent, no doubts, all-in ready before I make love to her.

The fact that she's willing to let me go says we're not quite there yet.

Disappointing as it may be.

"I'll miss you, boopsie-boo," I call as I exit the barn.

"Not like I'll miss you, honey nuts," she calls back, and I can't help laughing.

Ten minutes later, as I push through the door to my little cabin on the edge of Jace's property, Hope's still dancing through my thoughts. Half my brain is back in the barn with my wife. That's the only excuse for why it takes a full thirty seconds to realize I'm not alone.

But the three men scattered around my small living room, drinking my coffee and taking up all the space on my second-hand couch and favorite La-Z-Boy are being weirdly quiet.

Almost like they've been lurking in wait to shout—

"Surprise," a deep voice rumbles from the couch, lifting his mug my way.

"You little shit," I say, my smile splitting my face.

Ignoring Ryan and Jace—those two are always up in my space—I tackle my baby brother. His military buzz cut is shorter and his neck even thicker than when he was in town for the wedding, but he looks good. Happy and healthy and practically busting the seams of his Marines tee shirt.

"Watch the coffee, asshole," Clint says with a grin while he dodges me.

Jace has my back, and he leaps on Clint with an uncharacteristically happy, "Dog pile!" and soon all four of us are wrestling on the ground like we're kids again.

"You didn't tell me you were coming back, turd," I say as I noogie the only brother I ever had a chance of shoving around. At least for a few years, until the baby of the family bulked up like a ripped Bulldog his freshman year of high school.

"Would have ruined the surprise, idiot." He grunts, rolls, and suddenly all three of us are pinned under Clint, me with my arm twisted, Ryan yelping about his spleen, and Jace shrieking to watch the nuts, because he and Olivia are definitely having more kids.

"Weaklings," Clint says with a grin.

He lets us all go, leaving us huffing and smiling and laughing as we climb to our feet. I give him a man-hug, because *fuck*, I miss him when he's gone.

I'm proud as hell that he's serving our country, but I wish he didn't have to do it in Japan.

"You came home," I babble. I'm still stuck on having him here, in person. It's like one of those homecoming videos on Facebook, except way the hell better.

"Last chance for me to actually be here for one of your bachelor parties instead of tuned in from halfway around the world." He thumps my back, which hurts, because dude doesn't know his own strength. I'm no weakling, either, but I'm not a Marine. "So don't give me any of this *I'm already married* bullshit. We're still having a bachelor party."

"I'll bring the booze," Jace says.

"Damn right. I got the party tricks." Clint grabs my end table and lifts it over his head one-handed.

Considering the thing weighs a couple hundred pounds, yeah, that's a party trick.

"I'll bring the strippers," Ryan offers.

We all look at him.

He grins, and we all crack up.

"Okay, yeah, I'll bring George," he amends. "My trash panda never got a bachelor party either."

"George has a private bachelor party every day," Jace says. "And you don't want to know what I caught him and Sticky Fingers doing behind my bar the other night. I had to shield the baby's eyes."

"Shameless trash panda," Clint says with a grin. "Where is the old boy? I brought him snacks from Japan."

Ryan reclaims his coffee. "Probably on the square. He's still holding out hope that Maud and Gerald will forget he's lurking in wait and toss their old pastries."

"Speaking of hope, let's talk about Hope," Clint says with a grin and a brow wiggle. "How's married life, old man?"

I slouch back against the La-Z-Boy with a smile.

Waking up with Hope in my arms?

That was perfect.

I shrug. "Can't complain."

"Of course you can't," Jace says. "No man getting newlywed nookie can complain."

"Ain't that the truth." So technically I could probably lodge a complaint.

But I won't. Just because Hope's still skittish doesn't mean Operation: Real Romance won't succeed.

I'm a patient man.

I *will* win over my wife.

"I highly approve of all nookie," Ryan announces. "Newlywed and post-newlywed and pre-newlywed. Anything without a raccoon interfering is good."

Clint rolls his eyes. "Back to the bachelor party before you all get too graphic. So. Me. You three bozos. George. Who else?"

"If George is coming, Chewpaca should too," I tell them.

We all look at Jace.

"No way. I'm not bringing Princess and Duchess to a bachelor party. That's way too rough for them. They're tiny."

"Agreed," Clint says. "No hedgehogs. They might fall in a beer glass."

"Poker night at Mom and Dad's place," Jace declares. "The four of us back together, Dad, my raccoon, Blake's new alpaca. It'll be perfect."

"Aw, man, Cassie loves poker night," Ryan says. "We should do a bachelor party with the ladies too. You know Mom'll read us the riot act if she's not invited."

Jace nods. "I'm down with that. Liv and the baby can come too."

"So you can cheat and have her read the cards?" I say, poking him in the ribs.

He slugs me in the arm. "I don't need to cheat to beat the pants off you."

"Hey, hey, break it up. We're all winners just for being back together again," Ryan points out.

"Puke," Jace says, but he's grinning as he adds, "you're such a sap."

"Total sap, but fuck, I missed you assholes." Clint grabs us all in a group tackle-hug again. "Poker night bachelor party. Tomorrow night. Cancel your other plans, boys, because I'm only here for four days."

"Damn," I mutter.

Jace's phone dings, and though we could tease him about being attached to it, waiting for new baby pictures every time he's apart from Olivia for more than half an hour, instead we all lean over to look, because Clover is adorable.

But while it is Olivia who's texting him, it's not a baby picture.

And the message—*Trouble at goat yoga. Star just texted me. Are you with Blake? I think Hope needs help. Urgently.* —has me on my feet and flying back out the door.

FOURTEEN

Hope

The square is packed with excited citizens of Happy Cat, young and old, who've joined us on the warm spring morning to roll out their mats and do yoga with the baby goats.

We're inside a temporary fence so our four-legged friends don't run off. And while I'd love to be in downward dog with the twenty-five happy yogis warming up with sun salutations, I'm busy supervising the kids scampering over their backs and bottoms, handing the giddy baby goats carrots when they get too interested in ponytails and moustaches.

Hoof massages with a side of adorable are one thing.

A haircut or a 'stache trim by baby goat, however, is not what any of these Zen-seeking citizens signed up for.

Sadly, I don't realize the flaw in my carrot treat plan until it's too late.

One minute, I'm giving Vinnie Van Goat a carrot. The next, George Cooney, the world's most gluttonous pet raccoon, is charging through the temporary fence, shaking off the orange netting stuck in his back paw as he snatches a baby carrot from Biscuit the Kid's mouth.

Poor Biscuit rears up in surprise, which would be one thing if he weren't standing on the fire chief's back. But he is, and a beat later he's sliding down her neck, making Jessie flinch as he somersaults onto the grass with a bleat of terror.

And following the law of Baby Goat Chaos Theory—when one kid goes down, they all go down.

Or off-their-rockers in panic, as it were.

"George!" I shriek as he takes off after another goat, who has dropped his carrot and is running in hysterical circles in response to Biscuit's alarm.

His lordship the trash panda flips me off—I swear he does—and scampers around what's left of the enclosure, making yogis and goats scream. He tosses aside mats and knocks down more of the fence in his quest for baby carrots, careless of the Zen and property he's destroying as he literally steals snacks *from the mouth of babes.*

"George, STOP! Bad raccoon! *Bad!*"

When did the little beast get so fast?

How is he so fast?

He's the size of three normal raccoons, but he's dashing around like he's half-cheetah, and of course the babies are freaking out in response. In nature, a predator of George's size would be big enough to pose a survival threat to little goats, especially if he came crawling around with a few hungry friends.

George wouldn't hurt a fly—he's after the carrots, not the babies—but the little guys don't know that. They're acting on instinct and instinct is apparently telling them to hurl their tiny bodies at me, the yoga class, the fence, and anything else that might possibly offer protection or shelter.

"George, please," I beg as Star, the yoga teacher, implores her class to, "Take a deep breath, and let it out with a call for peace."

But no one is listening. To either of us.

The yoga class is on their bare feet, dodging flashing hooves, and George is in a carrot-feeding frenzy.

Normally, he's far too lazy and spoiled to actually hunt for his food. But I guess being on an ice chip and cricket diet since his run-in with the peanut butter has made George hangry.

And hangry George is actually kinda terrifying.

People are screaming, while Jessie tries to help me catch the rampaging trash panda.

But all too soon, I realize I have bigger problems. Namely—my baby goats are escaping, because George has destroyed the fence.

"No!" I shriek. I toss the rest of the carrots on the ground and take off, unsure which direction to start. The baby goats are even faster than George, and the streets of downtown soon echo with the frantic hoof beats of my runaway charges.

Passing motorists are honking, shouting, and weaving.

Terrified toddlers out for a pre-school field trip at the fire station squeal as Pepper crashes into their orderly line, tangling their toddler leash system.

"First things first, first things first," I mumble. Scanning my immediate surroundings, I spot a goat climbing into the slide and decide to start there.

I need to get my little buddies back into the trailer on my truck. One at a time.

Which is going to take forever. If I manage to get the job done at all.

There are goats all over downtown.

In the streets.

On the tables in the picnic area.

Digging up—oh, geez.

Ankle Biter's found a dildo that must've gotten buried under a pine tree during a prank last year, when the factory's products were used to litter the square. He's clutching it sideways in his mouth like an overgrown cigar and using it as a sword to fend off Widow MacIntosh, who's trying to corral him.

Actually—that dildo looks awfully familiar.

It could be Dildo Shaggins's older cousin. In blue, instead of purple.

I shake my head, because *not the time, Hope.*

Especially now that I'm hearing sirens.

"Oh, no." I clutch the kid I've just pulled from the slide tunnel, where he was curled up in a trembling ball, to my chest and stand, scanning the square.

There, on the other side, is a sheriff's cruiser pulling up in front of the yoga studio.

"I've got one," Star says breathlessly, trotting across the playground with Mickey, a white baby goat with mouse ear markings in black on his back. She follows my gaze, her smile falling away as she sees the flashing lights. "Oh, no. I'm going to get a ticket for violating my permit and letting goats run wild all over downtown. Aren't I?"

"No, you're not," I promise, panting from the running and the adrenaline and the worry. "I'll tell them it's my fault."

"But it wasn't your fault. It wasn't anyone's fault. It was just what the universe had planned for this morning.

Raccoon chaos and a goat chase." She shrugs. "This is why we practice staying in the moment. So we're ready for whatever comes next."

"You sound like Olivia," I say, nibbling on my lip as my mind races in frantic circles, proving I need more yoga in my life.

Or a shot of whiskey.

Or a Valium.

Or all three.

I would say a long run, but I had to give up training for a marathon last year when it made my energy field so strong that I shorted out the cash register at the grocery store.

Do *not* get between tired Southern mamas and Publix fried chicken on a Friday night. They will run over your feet with their cart and not even bother to bless your heart after.

Star beams. "Thank you! I adore Olivia. She and Clover come to my mommy and me class. They have the best energy. Like starlight and honeysuckle blossoms, you know?"

"I do." I eyeball her arms and decide she's got the biceps to handle two babies. "Here, take this little buddy too, and drop both of them off in the trailer behind my truck. I'll head the ticket off at the pass and hopefully grab another baby or two while I'm at it."

"Will do, good luck." Star flinches as I pass Biscuit into her arms, where he and Mickey greet each other with reassuring licks to each other's faces.

"You okay? Are they too heavy?"

"No, it's fine, I just got a little shock in my back pocket. I guess my phone is short-circuiting or something."

I wince. "Send me the bill for the new phone."

"But it's not your—"

"Trust me, it is my fault."

I jog away with a wave, heading for the deputy. He's a youngish guy I don't recognize at first glance, but he's got a no-nonsense gleam in his eye. I have to get to him before he reaches Star, and I need to take the heat. She barely makes enough teaching yoga to pay for her basic necessities. A ticket could mean the difference between grocery money and surviving on ramen for a month.

I wave a hand above my head, forcing a smile and willing my energy to simmer down. Instead, an electric feeling shoots up my arm and a moment later the streetlight above me shatters.

I squeal in surprise, covering my head with my hands as the glass rains down around me, fighting tears as a few shards break the skin at the back of my neck.

But it isn't the sting of the slivers digging in that makes me want to cry—it really doesn't hurt that badly—it's the certainty that my entire life is on the verge of spinning out of control, and that it will always be this way.

I will always be one electrical surge away from making something or someone explode. I will always be scrambling to fix the things I've broken and make it through another day without causing more damage than I can fix in the time allotted to me on this spinning orb. I will always be tired and stressed because being this weird thing that I am is exhausting.

Until Olivia gave my issue with electronics a name last year, and assured me it was totally normal, I assumed it was something I was doing wrong. But even knowing there are other people like me doesn't make it all better. I still have to deal with the crazy, and probably always will.

Sex would help calm your energy, Olivia's told me more than once.

Gently, of course, as only Olivia can.

But I'm not getting sex—I'm chasing goats and making lights explode in public.

I don't have any energy left to stop the tears filling my eyes from falling. I lift my head, sending them spilling over the edge of my lids to trace hot trails down my cheeks, and reach a tentative hand back around to pull the glass from my skin.

I'm still sliding slivers free, crying, waiting for the officer to reach me, while considering digging a hole in the sandbox and hiding there until my entire life goes away, when a familiar truck pulls around the corner from the fire station.

It's Blake's truck.

Pulling my bigger trailer.

And from the looks of it, there's someone sweet, fluffy, and very good with baby goats inside.

A sob of relief wrenches from my chest. I swipe my tears away and take a deep breath.

It's going to be okay. It's all going to be okay.

The officer stops beside me, casting a worried look at my blood-speckled hands as he asks, "You okay, miss?"

Blake already has Chewpaca on a lead, trotting down the trailer ramp, and the relief flooding me is so overwhelming, I feel more like dew-kissed spring grass stretching to wave good morning to the sun than a walking electrical disaster who never learned how to do love right.

"Yes, I'm fine, just a few scratches." I take a deep breath and brush away the tears. "And we're going to get the goats all gathered up, I promise." I motion toward Blake, who's leading Chewy down the sidewalk by the donut shop, where he instantly attracts Dorito, a tiny ginger goat who's often too bold for her own good. She emerges from the alley between the donut shop and the mortuary trotting after her surrogate alpaca father, wagging her little tail. "My husband brought rein-forcements."

My husband.

The words just slip out—warm and easy.

"Congrats on your marriage, by the way," the officer says. "The O'Dell brothers always make the water cooler gossip. Heard the wedding was memorable. Glad to see Blake so happy. He's a solid guy. Good friends with my oldest brother when they were in school. One of the only guys who didn't want to kick the little brother out of the pool when he came over to swim."

"He *is* a solid guy," I agree, cheeks flushing. "And thank you. I'm Hope, by the way."

He extends his hand. "Wesley Vance."

I wiggle my fingers and apologize. "I'm sorry. I would shake, but my hands are filthy." I'm feeling calmer, but Wesley has a lot of electronic stuff hooked onto his belt and there's no point risking further destruction.

"No worries." He smiles as he nods toward where Blake and Chewy have collected another wayward baby, proving my sweet alpaca truly is the Pied Piper of little goats, and my husband—*husband!*—is brilliant. "Are you sure you don't need help? It's slow at the station. I could call a few guys in for goat wrangling."

I blink. "You're not here to give me a ticket?"

He shakes his head. "Nah. We know it wasn't your fault. Ruthie May filled us in on the details when she called to report the goat in the bakery."

My eyes go wide. "There's a goat in the bakery?"

"Yep. Hiding under a booth apparently. Not in any rush to come out."

I sigh. "Okay, I'll go get that one personally. Thank you, Deputy. I really appreciate it."

"Thank your brother-in-law," he says with a wink. "Ryan's promised to buy the entire department drinks after work if we hold off on citing his raccoon. Again. He really should keep that rascal on a leash."

I nod as I back away. "George is so good with his hands, he'd probably slip right out of it. Thank you again."

He points to the shattered streetlight. "And I'll report this. Let me know if you need the paperwork for your insurance. I hope you aren't hurt too badly."

"I'll be fine," I promise, waving as I turn and trot toward the bakery. When I pass close enough to Blake and Chewy to be in hearing range, I shout, "Going to fetch a baby from the bakery. Get everyone else loaded into the trailer?"

"Will do." Blake flashes a thumbs-up.

"Thank you so much. You're my knight in shining armor."

My heart swells as he smiles.

"Me or Chewy?" he asks.

"Both, but mostly you." I blow an impulsive kiss, tummy flipping as he smiles even wider.

God, it would be so easy to get addicted to that smile.

To come to crave that combo of tummy flip and warmth spreading through my chest that only Blake has ever made me feel.

It would be so easy to fall madly in love with him and forget who I really am. Forget where I came from and all the lessons I learned growing up one of the casualties of a toxic marriage.

I could do it.

I could forget, but the amnesia would only be temporary.

Sooner or later, I would remember why marriage isn't for me. Maybe not in a year or two years, but eventually I'd start to feel trapped and it would make me crazy. I'd make Blake miserable, break his heart, and we'd end up hating each other even more than we did before we gave marriage another shot.

And I can't bear to have him hate me again.

Or even dislike me.

It's too perfect to be on his good side, basking in the glow of that sexy-sweet smile, knowing he's got my back and I've got his. I like being his friend. Love it, in fact.

It's almost as good as being the woman he loves.

Almost...

I fetch Honey from Maud and Gerald's bakery, apologizing profusely for the puddle my scared little kiddo left behind on their tile.

"It's fine," Maud says, already headed in with a wad of paper towels. "We all make messes when we're scared, and she's a sweet little girl. I'm sure she just wants her mama."

"I've got her uncle outside," I say, tipping my head toward the square. "I'll get her over to Chewy and she'll calm right down."

"He's a lover, that one." Ruthie May's grin doesn't quite reach her narrowed eyes. "But don't rush off so fast, honey. You've got to tell us all about your wedding day! What on earth happened? I've heard bits and pieces of the story, but nothing I can put together to make good sense."

I freeze, sweat breaking out along the valley of my spine as I remember how important it is that Blake and I make sense to Ruthie May.

If Kyle and Dean can't prove conclusively that my marriage is a sham, they're coming to her for any hint of marital discord. I have to keep her gossiping on the side of *Blake and Hope are so in love*, so Chewy can stay home with me and his BFF and goat babies where he belongs. I don't know if gossip is admissible in court, but in Happy Cat, Ruthie May's word is gospel.

I've got to say something, and I've got to make it good.

But my head has suddenly gone blank.

I genuinely cannot come up with a series of words to string together to save my life. I'm on the verge of stammering out a lame excuse and bolting for the door, when the bell tinkles behind me, and I catch Blake's smell drifting through the sugar-scented air.

Hmmm...I'd take him over cinnamon buns anytime.

I turn to him with a tight smile. "Ruthie May was just asking for our wedding day story," I say. "Says she hasn't heard one that makes sense yet."

He flashes Ruthie May a grin before fixing his gaze on me, the look in his eyes making my panties melt and my heart leap out to beat on my sleeve.

"That's funny," he drawls as he wraps his arms around me and Honey. "'Cause I've never heard anything that makes more sense than me and you, baby."

And then he kisses me, a just-barely-fit-for-public-consumption kiss that, even with a baby goat squirming between us and Ruthie May, Maud, and Gerald looking on, makes me feel like we're the only two people left on earth.

It's just me and this man who I'm beginning to realize will always own a piece of my soul. No matter where we go from here or how many years stretch out between now and the day we finally go our separate ways.

And maybe that's okay, as long as I leave a piece of his soul better than it was before I found it.

I emerge from the kiss bleary-eyed, but clear in my heart. I need to do something nice for this man, something very nice, to show him how much he means to me. And I have a pretty good idea what will put a smile on his face.

"Well, well," Ruthie May says, clearly pleased by the performance. "My gossipy side still wants details, but all in all it looks like this is a pleasant surprise for everyone involved."

"Except the goat," Gerald says, as grouchy as ever. But even he sounds like he might be a little touched, and when I look his way he's got his arms around Maud, patting her hip with obvious affection.

But Maud and Gerald spend their share of time fighting too. Sometimes here in the bakery, arguing over who burned the muffins or who keeps shoving more trash in the can instead of emptying the bag.

Last week, their shouting match was enough to get the Happy Cat sheriff's department involved. Or at least the deputy who lives next door.

All over whether or not to buy a new dryer.

A bird had pooped on Gerald's boxers while they were hanging out on the clothesline, and he decided he'd had enough of conserving energy, while Maud insisted birds wouldn't poop on his boxers if he'd wear the tight kind that make a smaller target.

That's the kind of marriage I don't want. The only kind I've ever seen, where even people who sometimes look happily married can be miserable underneath.

The reminder is enough to make me pull away from Blake and step toward the door. "We've got to get the babies home. See y'all later."

"Later," Ruthie May echoes, "but I still want details!"

"Let's just say we both finally ended up where we were supposed to be," Blake says with a wink tossed over his shoulder.

Ruthie May and Maud both swoon.

"You think she bought it?" he murmurs as soon as we're clear of the bakery and approaching his truck.

"Hook, line, and sinker," I say. "You're very convincing."

"Why don't you sound happier about that?"

I look up at him. "Of course I'm happy about it. And so grateful. You've been flat out heroic today."

"You liked my breakfast sandwich that much, huh?" he asks in a flirty voice that I answer with a serious one.

"Your breakfast sandwich was delicious, but I'm talking about bringing Chewy to the rescue. And listening hard enough last night to know that it was exactly the right thing to do. Most people wouldn't have remembered that I mentioned the babies like Chewy. But you did."

"I listen when you talk." He rests a hand at the small of my back, making my traitorous body hum all over. "You make me want to pay attention."

"And you make me want to say thank you with something better than words."

The confession slips out before I realize my traitorous tongue is flapping, so I punch the crosswalk button as an excuse to put distance between us.

I can't keep letting him touch me or I'm never going to make it through our marriage without climbing him like a tree. A really sexy tree. Every brush of his fingers over my skin is a wave sweeping onto the shore, eroding my resistance like grains of sand, helpless in the face of the tide.

"Meet me for sandwiches at the Kennedy Family Day School at six?" I ask as we cross the street toward his truck and the big trailer, where Chewy is already tucked safely inside. "I should have my surprise sorted by then."

"I thought you were going to let me cook for you."

"I think you deserve a treat tonight, and since my

cooking is far from something to write home about, I'm going to treat you to a Kennedy School feast." I stop by the trailer's gate to open it and let Honey scamper inside to take the ride home with her favorite Uncle Chewpaca. As expected, she practically dances over to meet him, wagging all over, probably telling him all about her harrowing adventure in the land of UnderDaBakeryBooth.

I count the goats, and breathe a sigh of relief.

We have them all. Thank goodness. And George is gone, leaving a mess that the yoga class is almost finished picking up.

"I like your cooking, but I'll take a gourmet sandwich treat too." Blake puts an arm around my waist. I start to pull away, but he leans in, murmuring into my ear. "Better kiss me, Mrs. O'Dell. Our shadow is over by the playground."

"Oh," I whisper, wrapping my arms around his shoulders, more relieved for the excuse to give in to the chemistry simmering between us than I should be. And then we kiss, and I'm even more grateful. And warm. Tingling all over, my soul dancing in my chest just like Honey danced, because that's what we do when we're close to someone special.

We tingle and soar and dance.

Sometimes without moving a muscle.

"See you at six." He presses a final kiss to my temple that makes me spin a little higher.

"See you then." I turn to walk away, so dazed that I don't think to look toward the playground until I'm halfway to my truck.

When I do, there's no sign of Dean.

I spin back to Blake to find him watching me go with a shameless grin. I prop my hands on my hips, feigning anger, but he just laughs—a head tossed back, throat exposed laugh that makes me want to run back and bite him in the sexy way—before saluting me and sauntering toward the driver's seat.

He's made the same gesture countless times, but today, it feels different.

Today, *I* feel different.

And tonight, I'm going to show him.

FIFTEEN

Blake

She's all I can think about the rest of the day, even while I'm trying to enjoy hanging out with Clint, who has no qualms about razzing me about my wife.

But I don't care.

Every minute until I get to see her again crawls by with aching slowness. Like watching paint dry in a monsoon.

I want her so fucking much.

And not just her body—though I want that too. Desperately. But I also crave her company, her smile, and her trust. Most of all I want a sliver of her faith, just enough to convince her that we should give this till-death-do-us-part thing a real shot. If I can get her to believe in me, in us, even a little bit, I know I can carry us both the rest of the way.

I'm at the Kennedy Family Day School, an old school that kept its name when the new owners turned it into a general store and restaurant, ten minutes early, eager as hell and not ashamed to show it, but I've barely settled into a rocker on the porch when Lizzie, the owner, sticks her head out the screen door. "Hey, Blake. Hope was just here."

My welcoming smile morphs into a brow pinch as I glance down at my watch.

"Oh, no, you're not late," Lizzie says, pushing through the door, a picnic basket hanging from one arm. "She was early. And she's got plans for you." She glances pointedly at the basket. "She ordered all your favorites and told me to tell you to meet her at your tasting room." She winks. "I guess she's in the mood for wine, good food, and some alone time with her hubby. Can't say I blame her."

Alone time.

Damn, that sounds good, and the hope filtering into my chest feels even better.

Maybe my reluctant bride is coming around.

And maybe tonight will be the night I finally get to show her how much she means to me.

I wouldn't object to spending several devoted hours worshipping every inch of her perfect self.

Operation: Real Romance is about winning her over heart, mind, and soul first, but physical intimacy is a part of that too. When I finally get to make love to her again, I'm going to make sure she realizes I'm in this with every part of me.

"Thank you," I say, accepting the basket and backing toward the porch steps. "We'll probably be back for cinnamon rolls tomorrow morning."

Lizzie laughs. "Aren't you even going to check and see what she ordered for you guys?"

"Nope," I say cheerfully, beeping open the truck. "Whatever it is, the sooner I get to my girl, the better it will taste."

I slide into the cab, setting the basket in the passenger's seat. It's not easy, but I force myself to go slow until I reach the edge of the Day School's gravel lot and pull onto the narrow country highway. And then I put the pedal to the metal, racing through the golden evening light to get to my wife.

Ten minutes later, I'm parking beside Hope's truck outside my brand-new and sadly as-yet-unused tasting room. It's built of Georgia pine, so fresh it still smells incredible. You can catch a whiff of it from the parking lot, clean and crisp, like a splash of gin in a warm wooden cup.

I had that once, with Clint, who started drinking it that way after one of his deployments. He's been all over the world, my baby brother. I used to be a little jealous, but lately it feels like everything I could ever want is right here in Happy Cat. It was so good to spend the afternoon walking my vineyards with him today, and I can't wait for the bachelor party tomorrow night, but much as I love and miss my brother, right now there's only one person I'm truly dying to see.

I bound up the stairs, picnic basket in hand and a smile on my face, even before Hope opens the door wearing a tight pair of jeans I haven't seen before—but which I like, a lot, a whole lot—and a white buttonless blousy top sheer enough that I can just make out the outline of her bra through the cotton.

It's a lace bra and one of those half-sized cups that do more plumping than covering, and it's damn hard to rip my gaze away from her chest.

"See something you like?" she asks.

"Um, yes. Very much," I say, biting my lip as my face goes hot. Fuck. Caught in the act.

"Which one?"

"Uh..." I frown. It's an unexpected question, but I'm game. "I don't know. I guess I'd have to see them both up close to be sure."

She circles her arm. "Then come on in and let's unwrap them."

I frown harder. "Unwrap them?"

"The sandwiches," she says, cocking her head with a chuckle. "What did you think I was talking about?"

I grin harder, and my grin isn't the only thing feeling hard. "The sandwiches. What else?"

I step past her, taking in the orange sleeping bag spread out in the middle of the floor, in between the two tasting bars and the two communal tables, where I have dreams of pouring drinks for as many as twelve people at a time if my license is ever approved.

"I set up an indoor picnic." She bites her lip like she's afraid I won't like it. Or possibly like she's afraid of something else. "It's nice enough to have it outdoors, but fewer bugs in here, and I thought maybe we could open a bottle of wine to celebrate."

I turn to her, relief and sadness rushing through me in equal measure. I'm glad Chewy's safe, but I'm not ready for this marriage to be over, not by a long shot. "So Kyle signed the paperwork?"

Her brow furrows before she shakes her head with another laugh. "Oh, no. No, he didn't. He's still being a dick, and I'm pretty sure Dean was trying to take pictures through the kitchen curtains today with one of those long telephoto lenses. Guess he really wanted a snapshot of me sneaking a mid-day hot chocolate as reward for getting all the baby goats back to their mamas in one piece."

"I'll break that for him when we get home." Anger

strikes in my chest like a match catching. "Teach him an important lesson about respecting a woman's privacy."

She waves a hand through the air. "No, it's fine. I'll just get some thicker curtains in there. Ones that will stay closed." She smiles. "I don't want to think about Dean or Kyle. This is a celebration night. Rick is going to feed all the animals for me so we can linger as long as we want."

"Sounds amazing." I set the picnic basket down on the edge of the sleeping bag, admiring the fresh cut flowers she's placed in a mason jar in the center. "This is beautiful, by the way."

"It's just a sleeping bag and some wildflowers. I didn't have time for much more by the time I got done running errands."

"It's beautiful," I insist, holding her gaze, hoping she knows I'm talking about so much more than the flowers.

She bites her lip again and glances away with a grin, and I can't help feeling a little proud of myself for making her blush.

"So what are we celebrating if not alpaca freedom?" I ask, stepping closer.

Her gaze returns to mine, the light in her eyes enough to stop my heart. Thankfully, her smile restarts it again with a firm tha-dump as she says, "Why don't you pour us a glass of wine and I'll tell you."

"All right." I nod, clapping my hands together as I start toward the bar on the left. "What are you in the mood for? White, red, or pink? We can open something to start and I can always grab something else if we decide our first choice doesn't pair well with the food."

"Ooo la la, so fancy." She slides up to the customer side of the bar as I step behind it, grabbing a wine key and placing it on the smooth wooden top. "Pink, I think. That's the one in the little fridge, right?"

"Yeah. And good choice. Most people look down on a pink wine, but the new ones are floral and fruity without being too sweet." I turn, reaching for the fridge handle. "And this one is..." My hand drops to my side and my words trail away as I see the framed paper sitting atop the fridge. I spin back to Hope, my stomach going tight. "Is that what I think it is?"

She smiles and claps her hands. "Surprise! You're ready to open for business, Mr. O'Dell."

"Oh my god." I release the breath I've been holding for the past two months, as it began to look like I might never be approved to serve liquor as long as Gary was head of the Department of Revenue. Or, as I'd come to think of it lately, the Department of Fuck-With-You. "Thank you. So much." I jog around the bar, pulling her into my arms for a hug.

"You're so wel—" Her words become a squeak as I lift her off her feet, swinging her in a circle before setting her back down and pressing an impulsive kiss to her cheek.

"No, seriously," I say in a softer voice as that electricity that's never far away when we're together crackles to life between us. "I appreciate this so much."

"Well, you were my hero today. It only seemed right to return the favor." She sways closer as I wrap my arms more tightly around her waist. "And I *did* make a few vows the other day."

My heart pitter-patters again at the mention of our vows.

Does she mean it?

That our vows meant something to her?

Is she finally seeing me? Trusting me?

"Blake?" she whispers while I search her beautiful

brown eyes with the soft honey flecks, looking for a deeper meaning to her words.

"Yes, my lady-hero?"

"Kiss me?"

That's one request I will never—*ever*—deny her. Never again.

I cradle her head while I lower my lips to hers, intending to make every moment count tonight. I don't want to just make love to her body.

I want to make love to her heart.

To her mind.

To her soul.

I want this kiss, this touch, this press of our bodies, to show her that I'm here.

Forever and always.

Whatever she needs. Whenever she needs it.

Her fingers smooth up my shoulders to tease through my hair while I make a leisurely exploration of her mouth, coaxing low, happy hums from her throat while our tongues glide together, teasing and savoring instead of clashing.

She pulls me deeper into the kiss, and I follow, because I'll go anywhere with this woman.

She's had my heart since that moment in Vegas when she lifted sad eyes to mine and asked if I wanted to sit with a loser who couldn't finish what she started.

We'd been friends in high school, pretty good ones—attending the same float trips and lock-ins with various clubs—but I'd never seen her with her guard down. Never seen capable Hope St. Claire so vulnerable. I'd instantly wanted to fix everything for her, to be the reason she found her happiness again.

I'd wanted to make her smile—just once, to prove that there was still good in the world and she could find it.

That kiss though—that first kiss.

It was like my first sip of good wine.

Life-changing. Paradigm-shifting.

And I know she felt it too. We'd only had a couple of drinks at that point. It was the kisses—not the booze—that inspired her proposal mere hours later.

This kiss is the same.

No holding back. No worries about the past or the future.

Just the two of us, connecting so raw and deep that I feel her touch all the way to my marrow. She tugs on my tee, and I slip my hands under her top.

Her skin on my skin is just— It's like wine made from grapes grown on my own land, so singularly sweet, unique, and hard-won that I could never mistake them for anything other than mine.

Just like her.

And I only want more.

Her hands flatten over my stomach, and I break the kiss just long enough to pull my tee over my head while she dips her head and licks my chest.

"*Hope*," I gasp.

"Do me next," she orders.

I don't have to be asked twice, and I'm smiling while I grip the edges of her wispy shirt and lift it over her head.

"Peach," I say, tracing the edge of that glorious lace bra.

My tongue follows my fingers, and I let the sound of her ragged breath be my guide, taking liberties with lowering her bra straps while I lick every inch of her breasts above the cups.

She arches her chest up, offering me more, her hands gripping my hair and holding me right where I am. "Blake," she gasps, "take it off."

In a wink, I've unhooked her bra, and her breasts come free, those pert rosy nipples just begging for kisses.

"So damn beautiful," I murmur. "I've missed you two."

A breathy laugh slips through her lips. "They've missed you too."

I graze my teeth over her nipple, and her knees buckle. "*Blake.*"

"I've got you, baby." I help her to the sleeping bag and lay her on her back, kissing and stroking and indulging in that fantasy of loving her slowly all over.

Taking my time.

Learning her body again.

Whispering her name, letting her direct me, I help her out of those tight jeans and her matching peach lace panties, kissing my way down her legs, and back up again, until I'm worshipping her between her legs with my tongue. Her gasps get higher, her breath more ragged, until my bride comes undone with my name on her lips.

"I missed this pussy," I murmur as I kiss my way back up her body.

"She missed your mouth," she confesses shyly.

"Just my mouth?"

"So much more than just your mouth." She's barely speaking above a whisper now, like the words are physically painful, and I want to promise her I'll never hurt her ever again.

That I'll only make her feel good. Protect her and her animals.

Be the man she needs.

I don't know what's holding her back, but I'll love her until she's willing to tell me. And then whatever it is, I'll keep loving her.

I can't imagine ever *not* loving this woman again.

"Did she miss my Dildo Shaggins?" I whisper.

Hope laughs, her skin glowing, her eyes taking on a sparkle again. "You're way better than Dildo Shaggins."

"I don't know, he might have a quarter inch on me."

She pushes me onto my back and reaches for my button. "But you're so much thicker than he is," she says, reaching into my pants and stroking my aching cock, which is now preening under her praise too.

Yeah, eating her turns me on.

But this is about *her*.

Not the animal in my pants.

"Hope—" I gasp out as she circles my head with her thumb.

Her eyes lift to mine, full of vulnerability and need. "I want *all* of you tonight."

"I'm yours. All yours." And I'm already fumbling for a condom in my wallet, because though I could happily wait all night—despite what my cock currently thinks—I want to be ready when she is.

"You make me feel things I shouldn't," she says as she continues to stroke me, making my eyes cross while I resist the urge to thrust into her touch. "But I don't want to fight it tonight. I'm tired of fighting."

"You never have to fight it again, baby. Not with me."

"I believe you," she whispers, and then she takes the condom from me and rolls it down my length before swinging her leg over me and bending to kiss me while she takes me deep inside her.

Fuck, this is heaven.

Sheer fucking bliss.

I groan against the intense need to come just from being buried in her slick pussy.

"God, I missed this," she gasps as she lifts up and slides down me again.

"So much," I agree.

"Can't get enough."

"It's been too long, but never again."

I cup her breasts and press them together, then lick the seam as she rides me, and I can already feel her body gripping my aching cock.

I'm so ready to come, but I hold out until I feel the first spasms of her orgasm squeeze me tighter, and we come together in a sky full of fireworks, Hope straining, her neck long and her head tilted back, giving me the most glorious view of her ecstasy and making my release so powerful, I don't know if I'll ever quite recover.

She collapses onto me, panting, as the last of her tremors leave her, and I wrap my overcooked spaghetti arms around her. "I love you," I whisper to her.

Probably not the best timing, I realize, as she immediately goes stiff.

Fuck...

But I get it.

She's scared. I'm not sure why, but I want her to know she can trust me.

"Blake—" she starts.

"Shh." I stroke her back. "Don't say it. Don't feel like you have to. I just want you to know...I'm here for you. I don't need it back to give it. And you can pretend I didn't say it if that helps."

"Really?"

"Really." I stifle a yawn as she starts to relax against me again. "I just want you to know...that you're perfect. To me."

She is.

She always has been. Even when I was pissed as hell at her for bailing on our first marriage, when I had to come to her rescue doing odd jobs and pretend like it never happened, when I thought I was nothing to her, I still wanted her. Loved her.

But I'm not nothing to her.

I never have been, or we wouldn't be here.

She just needs time.

And I'll give her all the time—and orgasms—in the world.

For as long as she'll let me.

SIXTEEN

Hope

I wake up, and for a moment I have no idea where I am.

But my mind, accustomed to racing to fill in the blanks when I wake up in an unexpected place, quickly pops answers into the gaps in my sleep-fogged memory.

I'm on a wooden floor with only a thin barrier beneath me, my shoulder half numb from being smashed against the hard boards.

So there's only one place I could be—curled up in the pantry in my childhood home, the only place far enough away from my parents' master suite that I can't hear them scream when they had one too many old-fashioneds at a charity event or I broke a remote control again, causing their quiet feuding to erupt into something more violent.

Instantly I'm flooded with the hot-cold feeling of shame and anger mixing together beneath my skin and a sour taste floods into my mouth.

Because even though I know it's not my fault my parents seem to loathe each other, or even if it's my fault that I'm clumsy, I don't really know that at all.

I'm an only child, and not because Mom has fertility issues. I've heard her grumble beneath her breath often enough—wishing she'd waited until she was older to become a mother—to know I was probably an accident.

Or at least a less-than-welcome surprise.

And then, there were no more surprises or accidents.

No brothers or sisters.

Just me, alone, the only kid in a house filled with price-less treasures I was terrified to touch since I couldn't even look at a radio without it malfunctioning, and parents who apparently felt the same way about me.

The therapist I saw for a while, after I fried one too many university-owned computers, failed out of vet school, and was so low I couldn't see a way forward that wasn't tainted by failure and regret, thought my parents were prob-ably scared to mess me up. That's why they were so distant.

Neither of them had easy childhoods—Dad's parents were even chillier and more withdrawn than mine, and my mom's dad was an alcoholic so violent and unpredictable I was never allowed to meet him.

So they really had no idea how to do the happy family thing right.

But as a kid I didn't know that. I only knew that I was rarely held, rarely touched at all, and that it created a bone-deep hunger inside of me that could only be filled by one thing.

I was four years old the first time I held a puppy in my arms, a poor, wormy little thing I discovered crying in the ditch near our front gate.

Dad was sure someone had dumped it there on purpose,

hoping a well-off family would take pity on the starving creature, and resented being targeted. He hated being manipulated, and neither he nor my mother had a soft spot for animals—Gram didn't start her farm until later in life, and I never knew for sure if she liked the animals or if it was just a passing hobby—but for some reason I still don't quite understand, they let me keep it.

And love it.

And nurse it back to health.

And name it Jane, because at four I named everything Jane, even a boy puppy destined to grow into a massive golden mutt with the deepest bark you've ever heard.

And then Jane was joined by two kittens I found in a garbage can in second grade—Oscar and Weiner, because at eight that was hysterical—and by the time I graduated high school I had three dogs, four cats, and a ferret. All someone else's castaway creatures that I'd rescued from one miserable situation or another.

All creatures that I never hurt the way I broke microwaves and ceiling fans, who made me feel normal when I knew I was anything but.

I had a hell of a time rehoming them all before I went to college.

I didn't want to rehome them. I wanted them to stay in their cushy digs in the back yard, in the swanky shelters and play yards I'd built for them with my own two hands because Mom refused to have animals in the house.

But I knew my parents wouldn't take care of them. They would feed and water them, sure—they aren't monsters—but they wouldn't play with them, listen to them, or spend time soaking up all the priceless wisdom animals give away for free if you pay attention.

They wouldn't truly *care* for them so the best thing I could do for my fur friends was to find people who would.

Letting go of Jane was the hardest. He was so old by then, rickety in his bones and so sore some mornings I had to squat down, leverage both hands under his hips, and deadlift his one hundred and fifty-pound body into an upright position. But I finally found someone wonderful—a CrossFit teacher a few towns over who let him hang out at the gym with him and his buddies all day and fed him way too many treats—and I let him go.

Because I loved him.

Utterly. Completely.

Unselfishly.

As I push into a seated position on the hard floor where Blake sleeps peacefully on the sleeping bag beside me, there are tears in my eyes. Even though I know by now that I'm not a little girl anymore—I'm not trapped in the pantry or in a house where I can't beg, borrow, or steal enough love to keep from starving—I'm still haunted.

My mother's second voicemail today didn't help.

I'm letting them down again and embarrassing them and causing *headaches* that could be handled *so much better*, according to her.

All this time, since the morning I woke up in Blake's bed in Vegas, and realized I'd gotten married in a pheromone-wasted stupor, I've been telling myself that it was a mistake because I don't believe in marriage.

I am anti-marriage and Blake is pro-marriage, a simple formula that explains why it can never work between us.

Horse plus cow can never equal goat.

It's against the rules of nature.

But here in the dark, with nothing but the two of us and a big empty room filled with the echoes of all the sweet things we did together a few hours ago, there's nowhere to hide from the truth.

It isn't that I'm anti-marriage. It's that I'm terrified to let him love me.

I don't know how to *be* loved.

Even if he were the kind to be happy with something more casual—a girlfriend or a friend with benefits—I still would have pushed him away.

Because I learned the hard way what it's like to beg for love and be denied, to hurl myself at the shut doors of my parents' hearts again and again until I was bruised all over, and to keep going back for more punishment because I was a child who needed love like I needed air. I needed their arms so badly it took years of dutiful snuggles from Jane before I felt anything close to okay.

And I know I could come to need Blake's arms even more, so much that, if he decided to let me go—and he would, because I never learned how to love any better than my parents did—it would destroy every tender thing left inside of me.

I would fall and fall and never quit falling.

The thought of that deep, dark hole of guilt and ineptitude, the one that would suck me in and devour me for the rest of my life, wrenches a sob from my throat. I smash a fist to my mouth, holding my breath as Blake stirs, mumbling sleepily as he rolls onto his other side.

But after a moment, it's clear he's still asleep.

I wait another long minute, ears ringing and heart racing in the loaded silence, and then I quietly dress, putting everything on except my shoes, which I hold in my hands until I've shut the tasting room door softly behind me. It isn't until I'm almost to my truck, however, that I realize I left my keys inside, somewhere in the darkness where they will be impossible to find without disturbing Blake.

And I can't fathom going back into that tasting room right now, back into that place that will always be home to one of my most beautiful memories and a terrible, stinging sadness. It will forever be the place where I realized how broken I still am, how broken I will probably always be.

Because better to be broken than tumbling forever through infinite sadness.

"Isn't it?" I ask, hot tears spilling down my cheeks, but going cold before they reach my chin. The spring night is cool, almost chilly.

The perfect night to run away from my problems.

Even though I know they'll chase me to the ends of the earth.

They always have, but this time, I won't drag Blake down with me.

Any more than I already have, anyway.

Without another thought, I jog off through the fields, taking the shortcut from Blake's place to mine. It's five minutes by road, but not much more by foot. Half the time, he'll walk over to fix my toaster or patch up my hard drive, if the job is small enough that he doesn't need his big toolbox.

But not anymore.

We can't be anything to each other anymore.

Not even friends.

I'll have to figure out an excuse to send myself away on a business trip for the rest of our fake marriage. Maybe to study that sustainable farm in Vermont I've read so much about, the one with the foreman who told me I could come shadow him any time and learn how to turn my shelter into a source of farm-fresh food for my community.

Kyle knows I've been obsessed with that place for a

while now. Maybe he'll believe that I love sustainable agriculture enough to tear myself away from my new hubby.

And if he doesn't...

Well, then we can fight it out in front of a judge.

I might not know how to love a human mate, but I've made a promise of forever to innocent creatures who won't leave.

Animals die, but they never willingly *choose* to abandon you. They never wake up one morning, stop loving the person who has cared for and adored them, and decide to make that person's life miserable, instead.

Animals take your love and keep it safe.

Safe.

That's what I want. What I need. Just to be safe again. Alone, and lonely sometimes, but good enough on my own to get by and have some fun while I'm doing it.

But when I stumble in the front door, I don't go to my bed. I go to the couch and fall onto the pillow Blake left there, inhaling his soapy, sexy Blake scent as I cry myself back to sleep.

And in the morning, I'm awakened by a loud pounding on my door, Kyle's voice shouting—"I've got proof, Hope. Time to admit your marriage is a joke and sign that animal over to me."—and I am reminded that things can always get worse.

Always.

SEVENTEEN

Blake

She's gone.

I'm not surprised—a part of me even expected it.

It's the reason I laid awake for so long last night, memorizing the feel of her in my arms, the sweet smell of her, the way her heart beat perfectly in time with mine.

Because my gut warned that she might be gone by morning.

Hope didn't say "I love you" back.

I get it, and I don't blame her or resent her for not saying things she isn't ready to say, but the fact that she didn't share her feelings with me remains significant.

I believe she feels what I feel. I know she does. The way she touched me last night, kissed me, held me like she couldn't bear to let me go, not even for the few minutes it took to fetch the extra sleeping bag from my truck so we'd have something to cover up with while we slept, matters too.

It matters enough to send me bolting out the door without bothering to clean up the remains of our picnic or roll up the sleeping bags.

Because I have to find Hope and convince her that she doesn't have to run from me. I'm a patient man. I'm willing to give her as much time and space as she needs to feel comfortable letting me the rest of the way into her heart. Tending a vineyard for years before my vines finally started to bear enough fruit to make something delicious has taught me that good things are worth waiting for, working for.

And Hope isn't just good. She's incredible.

I just wish I could make her see it.

I race out to my truck, thrown by the sight of Hope's old beater still parked beside it. Maybe she walked back to her place.

Or sleepwalked?

Shit. If she was sleepwalking, there's no telling where she is.

"Hope?" I call.

No answer.

I pick up the pace and circle the tasting room, looking for any sign of her and finding nothing.

And now I'm hoping she *did* run away.

At least then I'd know she was safe.

I dash into my truck and speed along the country roads, fear gripping my heart.

I don't have double locks on the tasting room. And we didn't lock it at all. If she was up sleepwalking, she could be hurt. Lost. Worse.

I tell myself Hope's a nature girl and more than capable of getting herself home in the dark, but I'm also thinking about all the ruts in the trail between our places, holes I'm going to fill in and cover with a fresh coat of gravel as soon as I ensure she hasn't sprained her ankle and ended up trapped alone in the woods overnight.

As soon as I verify she's okay.

She *has* to be okay.

I roar up to her place.

Dean isn't at his post. His station wagon is there, but it's empty and there's no sign of him in the pasture or beside the road.

My inner danger alert system is going overtime with warning signals when I rumble into the shelter's gravel parking lot to see a swanky Mercedes parked by the house.

Fuck.

Kyle.

I'm in no state of mind to deal with him right now. Not when I don't know where Hope is, or if she's okay.

I slam out of the truck, jogging around to the back of the house, hearing raised voices before the porch comes into view. And then I see them—Kyle on the steps, yelling at a frazzled-looking Hope—*thank god* she's safe—while Cara and Dean stand in the grass nearby.

Dean's holding Chewy on a lead while the alpaca nibbles anxiously on the rim of his baseball cap. For his part, Dean is grinning like getting a hat chewing from a high-class alpaca is the best time he's had in a while. Cara is chattering, but after my one and only run-in with her, I don't have any clue what she might be saying, and I don't care.

Because the St. Claire cousins are swiftly headed toward some kind of nuclear explosion.

I have to put a stop to it.

And hug my wife.

Because she's safe.

I charge up the steps, startling Kyle enough to make him stumble. He grabs for the railing to steady himself, while I grab for Hope, pulling her into my arms and hugging her tight.

"They're taking Chewy," she sobs into my neck.

"He's rightfully mine," Kyle says.

"The hell he is," I snap, glaring at him over Hope's head.

"They're taking him because you slept at the winery and I slept here," she says, breath catching as she clings tighter to my shoulders. "I tried to explain but they won't let me and I—"

"Shh, it's okay, baby," I promise, cradling her head in my hand, fingers snagging in her tangled hair. She's a mess—still in last night's clothes with her hair wild and her eyes puffy from crying.

And she's beautiful. Perfect.

"Husbands and wives sleep together," Kyle declares with a sneer. "Any court of law—"

"Hasn't fucking declared you the owner of that alpaca, so you can just hand him back over right *now*."

Fury courses through my veins.

I don't get pissed.

But I'm fucking *livid* right now.

Kyle doesn't seem to realize he's in danger. "You're wasting everyone's time, *and* you're costing me money. The courts call it abandonment. You won't win, so stop trying to convince us this marriage is real."

"You think this isn't real?" I'm clinging to Hope so I don't put my fist through Kyle's face. "I. Love. This. Woman. And on top of that, who the *fuck* gets married *just* for an alpaca? No one. That's who. So don't stand there telling me my marriage isn't real. It's as real as the sun coming up in the morning and as real as you being a pompous asshole who only cares about money."

"He cares about his elephant dick too," Cara calls. "And so do I."

We all momentarily gape at her, and Hope, who's gone completely still in my arms, sob-shouts, "I have a UTI!"

Kyle swings back around. "*What?*"

"Baby—" I start.

"If you'd let me explain," she continues, twisting in my arms to glare at Kyle, "I could have told you before why I left Blake at the winery. I woke up in the middle of the night in pain and had to come get medicine."

"Ugh, UTIs are the worst," Cara says. "I get one every time I have too much sex."

"*Exactly*," Hope says.

We all pause again, once again looking at Cara.

"Cara, go wait in the car," Kyle snaps.

"So if sex is how you judge a marriage," I say, "and *my* wife is getting an infection from too much sex, and yours isn't..."

"We're having *so* much sex." Hope swipes at her eyes, her voice getting stronger. "Sex in the shower."

"Sex on the floor," I add. "And on the kitchen counter."

"And in your truck."

"And *your* truck."

I scrub a hand across my chin, pretending to search my memory before nodding as my temper cools and I relax into our story. Not too hard, since I've fantasized about making love to her all these places. "Yep, sure did. And in the stables."

"And the barn," she says, turning a watery grin up at me. "Totally worth the hay in tender places."

"And in the family bathroom in the square, and—"

"Okay, okay," Kyle says, propping a hand on his hip. "So

you've allegedly banged a lot. But you still slept apart last night, and that's admissible in a court of law."

She nods to me. "I told Blake to stay there since he had some work to do first thing."

I'm starting to catch on. "But I forgot my toolbox," I say, cutting in before Kyle can say something stupid, which, judging from the sneer still curling his lip, he's eager to do. "And good thing. If I'd come home to find you'd stolen our animal, I would have had to call the sheriff and that certainly wouldn't look very good for your case, would it?"

"You can't steal your own property," Kyle says. "And all I'm hearing is a bunch of lies and excuses."

"You think my wife's lying about having a urinary tract infection?" I ask, glaring at his pompous face.

"I mean, not to be gross about it," Hope adds, "but they do call it the honeymooner's disease for a reason."

"I want to see a doctor's note," he says. "Or at least a prescription."

"And I'd like you off our property before I have to go fetch my shotgun," I say pleasantly. "My wife's medical history is none of your business. And neither is our sex life or our married life or anything else. The only important part is that it's *real*." I squeeze her hand before letting it go and descending the steps slowly, giving Kyle plenty of time to dread the moment when I reach him.

Long before I even get close, he takes a step back, clearly reading the warning in my eyes.

"So here's what you're going to do," I say in a soft, but dangerous voice. "You're going to get off this land and stay off of it until you've learned to behave yourself and are invited to come back." I nod toward Dean. "And you're going to call off your detective and get him out of sight of our farm."

Kyle jerks his chin up. "I'll do no such thing. I have every right to—"

"You have the right to observe us while we're in a public place. You have no right to come onto our property without permission and take animals out of their pens. And you certainly have no right to camp in the Fricks' pasture. One call and they'll have the sherriff's department out here so fast Dean won't have time to roll up his yoga mat before he'll be cited for trespassing."

"I'm not technically in their pasture except to use the bathroom now and then," Dean pipes up, "but camping on the side of a public road *is* against the law in Happy Cat. I mentioned that to Kyle, but he said no one enforced those laws."

"Well, we can make sure they're enforced now," I say, casting a tight smile Dean's way. "My brother's a firefighter and real close with the local law enforcement."

Dean nods, glancing up at Chewy. "Well, I guess I'm ready to head out, then. He can keep the hat if you don't mind. It looks good on him."

Huh. Chewpaca stole Dean's hat while we were all arguing.

"It does, thank you," Hope says, relief in her voice as she hurries off the porch and past Kyle and me. She takes Chewy's lead from Dean, stroking the alpaca's nose as he nuzzles her neck in welcome and his tail begins to wag.

"That alpaca is *mine*," Kyle says.

"Then you won't mind proving it in court," I reply tightly. "Get. Off. Our. Property."

"C'mon, Kyle," Cara says. "Let's go see if we can give me a UTI while I can still get a prescription for antibiotics. I don't know what kind of medical care will be available while we're on safari."

"I *will* see you in court," Kyle mutters as he stalks off with Cara and Dean.

And I dash to catch up with my wife.

She's so precious, and I'm terrified I've scared her again.

I snag her hand as I reach her. "You okay?"

She sucks in a shaky breath and nods while we walk. "Yes. *Yes.* Thank you. You—you saved him. And me. Even though I probably don't deserve to be saved."

I pull us to a stop and turn to face her, Chewpaca beside us, and hold her gaze, waiting until I can feel her full attention fixed on me before I whisper, "I meant what I said last night. I love you. And that doesn't stop because you needed some space."

Her eyes fill with fresh tears and tension digs in between her brows. "But I ran away."

I nod. "I know. And I still love you."

She swallows, her throat working. "And I'm afraid."

"I know, me too," I say, the backs of my own eyes beginning to sting. This has been one hell of a morning already. "It's scary as hell. But it's worth it. *You're* worth it."

"No, I'm not." She blinks faster, sending fresh tears streaming down her already puffy cheeks. "I don't think I know how to love a human like this. I'm so scared, Blake. I'm scared you'll make me love you more than anything in the world and then you'll realize you've made a horrible mistake. I can't live up to this idea you have of me and I'll probably never be able to love you the way you deserve, and then you'll leave and I'll be so broken I'll never—"

"Hush." Heart breaking with a mixture of pain and relief—she does feel it too, this unparalleled pull—I draw her close, hugging her tight as I promise, "Baby, I'm never going to leave you. Haven't you realized that by now? Whether we're friends, enemies, lovers, or a mix of all three,

I'm going to keep coming back for more. I can't stay away from you. Even when I try."

She sniffs. "I don't want to be your enemy."

"And I don't want to be yours."

"And I don't think I can be just your friend," she whispers.

"Yeah, me either." I kiss the top of her head. "I want to get you naked too much."

She pulls back, gazing up at me with a worried look that isn't comforting, but it's honest and that's all I can ask of her. "And I think we should talk more. And maybe I should talk to someone else."

I frown. "Someone else?"

"Like a counselor maybe," she says, gaze cutting to the right.

"Yeah," I say, nodding my encouragement while Chewpaca nuzzles her hair like he's thanking her and telling her he loves her too. "If you think it will help, that would be great. And I could come with you, if you want."

Her attention shifts back to me, a wry smile curving her lips on one side. "You want to go to marriage counseling with your fake wife?"

"I want to go to counseling with the woman I love," I correct. "If she thinks it would help. God knows I'm not a flawless specimen."

"But pretty close," she says, wrinkling her nose. "As far as I can tell."

I brush her hair from her forehead. "Well, thanks. But I'm sure there are lots of ways I could learn to be a better partner to you. To give you what you really need instead of what I think you need, you know? And...listen better and shit."

She laughs softly. "That's the most important part, I hear. The 'and shit' part."

I grin. "Yeah, well, cut me a little slack, okay. I grew up with three brothers. I'm probably the most touchy-feely of all of us, but I'm still a dude raised with dudes. All the O'Dell boys are a touch feral."

Her smile falls. "Speaking of feral, I have a wild cat colony from over in Milledgeville due at nine and I still have to take a shower because right now I look like the Feral Cat Queen, not the woman who's going to turn their savage lives around."

"You're beautiful," I insist.

"I'm a mess," she says on a laugh. "But thank you for standing with me while I try to get a little less messy."

"It's an honor. Come on. Let's get this sweet boy back to his home so you can get a shower."

She looks at Chewpaca, who gazes back at her with utter adoration.

I'm the last person to believe in things like crystals and star charts, but for a second I channel my inner Olivia because I swear I see both of their auras light up with joy. Hope gives her entire self to the creatures in her care—body and soul—and in turn they love her with a trust and devotion I've never seen before. Not in an entire lifetime of growing up around country folk who love their pets like members of their family.

I want to make her light up like that someday, and I'm willing to do whatever it takes to make it happen.

Starting tonight, by showing her I want her to be a part of my life, even my belated bachelor party.

Especially a part of my belated bachelor party.

EIGHTEEN

Blake

I should be working at the vineyard—removing excess bud breaks from my vines—but I don't want to leave Hope or Chewpaca alone right now.

Thankfully, I have a trick up my sleeve.

Namely, my brother.

After a quick text, Clint shows up without question.

"Go work," he orders me. "I'm on alpaca guard duty."

"That's not necessary," Hope says, running a hand through her still damp hair. In addition to being sexy and sweet, my wife takes quite possibly the fastest showers known to female kind. Call me crazy, but I find that kind of efficiency hot.

But then, I find almost everything about her hot, lovable, or both.

"I can keep an eye on him while I work," she adds.

Clint pulls a Marine look on her, and if it's possible for a human body to stutter, that's exactly what hers does.

"I mean thank you," she says hastily. "Sir. Thank you, sir."

"Need anything?" I ask him. "Water? Sunscreen? Some palmetto bugs to snack on?"

He turns a glare on me.

The man's in full Devil Dog mode, and I've never been more grateful to have him as my brother.

"What can I help with?" I ask Hope.

She shakes her head. "After the feral cats arrive in about twenty minutes, I have a preschool group coming to visit, and a pair of miniature horses being delivered this afternoon. But Rick can help with the horses when he gets here. You have stuff you need to do at the winery. You can finally start planning opening day."

"It can wait."

"Really?" she presses. "You've already been delayed so long and I—"

"It can wait," I insist. "Clint and I are here for the day."

She casts a glance at Clint and pulls me a few feet away. "Can I confess that I find your brother just a teeny bit scary?" she whispers.

"Yes," I whisper back, "but he's on our side, and he's only scary when he has to be. Ask him about his pet frog sometime, but not while he's on alpaca guard duty. He doesn't like to get emotional when he's being all Marine-y."

"I heard that, asshole," Clint growls.

"That's his pet nickname for me," I add.

Even though she says she's fine, and even though Clint's on duty, I stick around the farm to help.

And I'm so glad I do. I get to watch her welcome her preschool group—a ridiculously cute assortment of small people—and lead them around the farm, telling them the stories about all the different animals, where they came from and how they contribute to the world and what everyone can do to give animals a safe place to live.

I love watching her relax and light up. And then she kneels down to hug a little girl who's afraid to pet the dogs, assuring her that she never has to do anything she doesn't want to do and the dogs' feelings won't be hurt, and my heart breaks open a little wider, letting more love inside.

She's such a damned good person. And knows so much more about love than she gives herself credit for.

I make a mental note to tell her I think she's an excellent lover of humans just as George makes an appearance, waddling into the pasture to take a turn on the baby goat slide before heading for the feed trough, earning himself a swift chasing-out by Chewpaca. Chewy snorts, and then emits a sharp cluck when George plops on his rump just outside the fence and chitters raccoon smack in the alpaca's direction.

"You have your own slide, George," I say. "Don't torment Chewpaca. Don't you need to be home? Go home for popcorn? Or supper? Something?"

He tilts his head at me, and a minute later, he waddles back toward the road.

"He keeps stealing the baby goats' veggie treats," Hope tells me with a nod at the raccoon as the preschoolers load up on their bus, giggling and making animal noises, making me think the field trip was a rousing success. Clint's still standing guard, but he hasn't disturbed the flow of the day. Sure, he made the teacher's aide sniffle a little just by looking at her, but the kids climbed him like a statue.

"I think he's taking presents to Sticky Fingers and the babies," Hope adds.

"He's a ladies' raccoon, isn't he?"

She laughs. "He's a one-lady raccoon, and Sticky Fingers has him wrapped around her fluffy tail. You hungry? I've got a frozen lasagna I can throw in the oven. Should be ready for dinner in about an hour."

"I have dinner plans for us," I tell her.

She lifts a brow. "Oh, you do, do you?"

"We're going to have a ton of food at the bachelor party."

Her brows inch even higher. "That's dinner plans for *you.*"

"No, for both of us. It's a bachelor party poker game at my folks' house. Cassie and Olivia are coming. Probably George too. We can bring Chewpaca. If you think he might want to celebrate with us."

She blinks once, then twice, and then throws her arms around me. "That would actually be amazing," she says. "I know I said Kyle wouldn't steal Chewpaca, but after today I'm not so sure. I talked to Mr. Ashford earlier, and he verified that since there's a dispute over which of us was married first, there's no legal precedent to rehome him without official paperwork, but...I think Kyle's getting desperate for closure."

I squeeze her tight. "Then Chewy comes with us tonight. I won't let anything happen to him. I promise."

Two other iron vices circle us, lifting us both off the ground. "I won't let anything happen to him either," Clint says. "Or you two. We're going to have the best bachelor party ever."

NINETEEN

Hope

I'm falling in love with my husband.

Or maybe I've always been in love with him, and I've just finally stopped fighting it.

Whichever it is, I should probably stop. Or start.

Stop falling or start fighting.

Instead, I push all the stressful thoughts to the back of my head and put on my cutest sundress—the soft blue one with the crisscross top that makes my modest chest look like something pretty special—strappy sandals, and earrings. Honest to god earrings, that I have to dig out of the back of my office junk drawer, where I tossed them in the middle of a work emergency after Jace and Olivia's wedding, which was the last time I was anything close to dressed-up.

But the look on Blake's face as I meet him in the kitchen after our separate showers is more than worth the effort.

His eyes go wide and his lips part, but no words come

out for a long time until finally he breathes out a soft, "Wow," that sends tingles racing across my skin and a smile bursting across my face.

"I can be a girl when I want to be," I say, fingers threading together in front of me as I fight the urge to reach for him. He also looks delicious, good enough to eat in a white button-up rolled at the sleeves and a pair of crisp khaki shorts. "You ready?"

"I'd rather stay here and get you out of that dress," he says. "But yeah. We should probably go. Clint texted and it sounds like everyone else is already there, getting their pre-game on. He's trying to save us a couple of his signature carne asada tacos, but isn't making any promises at this point."

I take the hand he holds out, but instead of starting for the door he squeezes my palm. "You okay with this? I was thinking in the shower and started worrying a party cele-brating our marriage might be more than you're up for after last night and this morning."

I shake my head. "Maybe it should be. But I'm excited to see everyone. And when the time comes to tell them the whole story, I truly think they'll understand. Is that naïve of me?"

"And what if the time never comes?" he asks, drawing me into his arms, making my pulse spike hard enough that I cast a worried glance overhead.

But the kitchen lights don't so much as flicker. Despite the drama of the morning and the pleasant stress of having twelve little ones to keep safe in my often-chaotic animal environment, today's been one of the calmest energy-field days in recent memory, making me think Olivia was right about sex working wonders for releasing excess electro-magnetic whatever.

Of course, fewer broken toasters isn't a reason to make a man promises you're not sure you can keep, but there's so much more to Blake than that.

More to *us*.

So I say, "Can we take it one day at a time? At least for a little while? I hear that's a thing that works for a lot of people."

He beams, like I've given him so much more than the sliver of a promise. "Sounds good. Especially if one day at a time leads to one night at a time." He steps closer, gathering me against him as he tips his head closer. "No pressure at all, but I would really love to make you come for me again when we get home."

I lift my chin, my lips prickling as they move closer to his. "I have zero objections to that plan. And I'd like to return the favor. I'm pretty good with my mouth too, if you remember from our first wedding night."

"Oh, I remember," he says, his voice going husky as his hands cup my ass, pulling me closer to where he's getting girthy again.

I sigh into him as his lips cover mine. "Don't ever put your cock on a diet."

He laughs softly. "That's not the way cocks work, snick-erdoodle."

"I figured, but good to get confirmation. 'Cause I love him just the way he is."

"Chubby and ridiculously eager?" he asks, backing me toward the sink.

"Don't talk that way about him," I say, breath catching as Blake's hands circle my waist, lifting me onto the kitchen counter with an ease that makes me feel like one of those delicate women who don't spend all day every day hauling bags of feed and showing bossy billy goats who's in charge.

"What are you doing?" I ask as his hands smooth up my thighs beneath my dress.

"Taking it one night at a time," he says, his fingers hooking in the sides of my panties.

"But we have to—" My words end in a moan as he kisses me, sweet and sexy and oh-so-steamy, pushing me from hungry to starved for him in ten seconds flat.

Before I fully realize what I'm doing, my shaking hands are working open the buttons on his shirt and he's ripping my panties down my legs. I just *want* him so badly.

His touch, his kiss. His body.

All of him.

He kisses a trail down my neck, while I fumble at the close of his shorts, and then he parts the crisscrossed fabric covering my breasts, drawing one already tight nipple into his mouth, and I ignite.

I am fire and he's gasoline and if ever I was going to blow up every appliance in my kitchen, this is it. But as he does magical things to my breasts with that talented mouth of his, and I thread my fingers into his hair and hang on for dear life, the only sparks are coming from the two of us.

From the way we make each other ache and need so much that by the time he finally slides the condom on and pushes inside me, I'm wild with wanting him.

Just him.

No past. No future. No baggage

Just two people who create magic every time we touch.

"Yes, please, Blake, don't stop," I beg as he takes me hard, his fingers digging into my hips as he drives between my legs and the tension building between us twists tighter. I can feel him trying to hold back, to be gentle, but I don't want gentle.

"Give it to me," I breathe, clinging tighter to his shoulders. "I want to feel how much you want me."

He groans. "I want you so much, but I don't want to hurt you."

"You're not hurting me," I say, nipping at his neck. "You're making me so hot and wet and—" I suck in a breath as he fucks me deeper, faster, until I'm so tangled up inside I know it's only a matter of time before I rip through the stitches still holding me together. "God, yes, please. More. Yes, yes! Oh, please, Blake, please. You feel so good."

"So good," he echoes, gripping my bottom in his hands and stepping away from the counter.

A sound of surprise and protest escapes my lips—we can't take a break now or I might spontaneously combust from despair—but then he shows me there's something even better than getting it on with my husband on the kitchen cabinets.

"Hold tight to my neck," he orders. As soon as I obey he uses his grip on my ass to rock us into each other, getting even deeper than he could before, slamming our bodies together with just enough of a naughty factor to make me feel deliciously wicked.

I come crying out his name and he joins me a moment later, his cock jerking inside me, drawing out my release until I'm punch-drunk and clinging to him like a spider monkey who's gobbled up one too many fermented cassava melons.

"Damn, woman," he says, collapsing on the chair behind him, with me still straddling his legs and his softening cock still buried inside me.

I fight to catch my breath with what I'm sure is a goofy grin. "Wow."

"Double wow," he echoes.

"That was so good," I murmur, stroking his hair. "Good Blake. Good alpha alpaca."

He chuckles softly. "Is it wrong I kind of like being petted like a good boy after sex?"

"No, that's normal," I say, continuing to smooth the silky strands from his face. "Because you are a very good boy."

He kisses my neck, rumbling against my skin. "Do I get a hubby treat?"

"You get all the hubby treats," I say. "You do that every time I come into the kitchen and I'll be making you gourmet meals in no time. Three courses. And dessert."

"Fatten me up?" he asks.

"Well, then your body would match my favorite part of you," I tease, grinning at him as he pulls back to shoot me a narrow-eyed look. "I'm just kidding," I say, patting his cheek gently. "It's not my favorite part."

"It's not?" he asks.

I shake my head, moving my hand from his face to the middle of his chest as I whisper the scariest thing I've said in a long time. "This is."

"My heart?"

I nod and he leans in, kissing me with so much love I know it will make me cry if he doesn't stop soon. But just as the waterworks are about to erupt, he pulls back and announces, "Time to go feed our bellies. Newlyweds can't survive on sex alone," almost as if he knows.

Knows that we're going to have to get there with baby steps.

But that he also has no doubt that we'll get there, one day and steamy night at a time.

TWENTY

Blake

You know those nights when you beg the universe to cut you some slack?

To ease up and let everything go smoothly for once in the history of your lovably insane family so you can impress the woman of your dreams?

And then you show up to your belated bachelor party to find a woman stranded atop her cupcake car, surrounded by a family of raccoons and sobbing into the cake boxes in her arms?

"Looks like tonight's going to be another one of those nights," I mumble beneath my breath as I drop the gate on the trailer and Hope hitches a lead onto Chewy's harness.

She follows the direction of my gaze, her eyes narrowing. "Oh, no. Poor thing. I'm beginning to think she and her cakes really are cursed." She sighs. "She must not know they're pet raccoons." She hands me the rope. "Take Chewy out back to meet everyone. I'll rescue the dessert delivery girl."

But before Hope can start down the line of cars parked in front of my parents' five-acre ranch, Clint jogs up the path from the house, shouting, "George Cooney, get your fluffy ass inside before Ryan kennels your entire family."

George's main squeeze, Sticky Fingers, stands on her hind legs and blinks her bright eyes at Clint, bringing her front paws together in an impressive begging display, but my brother's having none of it.

"Go on, get," he says, shooing the would-be cake bandits back toward the gate enclosing the backyard. "I'm serious. Mom and Dad used to raise show wieners. They've got a kennel plenty big enough for all of you."

"Show wieners?" Hope whispers, laughter in the voice.

"Miniature dachshunds," I confirm. "But growing up we called them the showeenies. One of Dad's many get-rich-with-a-side-gig ideas that turned out to be way more work than he bargained for. The vet bills alone almost broke him."

She hums beneath her breath as George chitters something serious-sounding. A moment later he and his entire family—Sticky Fingers and their three babies, who are plump adolescents by now—make a break for the back yard.

Atop the cake-mobile, the spiky-haired pixie lets out a shaky breath as she turns to Clint. "So they're not rabid?"

"Nope. Just a bunch of poorly behaved pets." He crosses to stand beside her passenger's side, reaching his arms up. "Here, let me help you down."

The woman visibly recoils, like she's encountered a rotted corpse instead of a buff Marine with green eyes nearly as pretty as mine. My mother told me I have the best eyes way too many times for me to believe it's anything less than the truth, which means his must be second best.

"No, I'll get down on my own," she says in a tight voice. Adding, "But thanks," as a none-too-friendly afterthought.

"All right," he replies, still amiable and welcoming. "Then how about the boxes? Want me to take those? Make it easier for you to climb off the roof?'

The woman shakes her head harder, backing still farther from his outstretched hands. "Oh, no. No way, I can't—" Her words end in a gasp of surprise as she pitches backward off the roof of her car.

Hope sucks in a breath, hand flying to cover her mouth, but exhales in relief a moment later as Clint lunges and saves her, catching her in the nick of time. Sadly, her boxes don't fare nearly as well. The tops of the white dessert containers fly open, spilling cupcakes all over the pavement as he draws the woman closer.

After an initial curse, she goes limp, allowing herself to relax into his arms. He sets her on her feet and curls a gentle hand around her shoulder, leaning down to say something I can't make out from this far away.

I angle closer to listen in, but Hope grabs the sleeve of my shirt. "She's already mortified enough, I'm sure, without knowing she had an even bigger audience. Leave them alone."

She winks, and I nod. "Fair enough."

I follow her to the shortcut to the back gate where Sticky Fingers and the teen raccoons are perched atop of the trashcans, peering over the edge of the fence at the scene unfolding by the street.

"You too," Hope says to the mama. "Leave them alone. And that goes for the people as well as the cupcakes. You don't need all that sugar. Remember what happened to George?"

At the word "cupcakes" Sticky Fingers bares her teeth in something a little too devious to be a smile, but that makes Hope laugh anyway. "Speaking of, where's George? He's not going after the cupcakes, is he?"

Sticky Fingers chirps at her.

"What did she say?" I ask Hope.

"She's a raccoon. I have no idea." She looks back over her shoulder. "But it doesn't look like he's near the cupcakes."

"He's probably going after the tacos," I point out, and she laughs.

Farther into the backyard, the party is in full swing. Mom and Dad are in the Jacuzzi, surrounded by tiki torches and clearly on the verge of making out post glasses of champagne. Up on the deck, the rest of the crew—Ryan and Cassie, Jace and Olivia and Clover, napping in a baby swing swaying softly back and forth at the urging of Olivia's bare toes—are talking and laughing and eating.

At least, until Ryan spots us. "Hey! It's the newlyweds! And only...seventeen minutes late."

Jace grins over his daughter's swing. "Pay up, old man."

"You were betting on how late we'd be?" Hope asks with a smile.

"Yeah, and frankly, I'm sorry for you that you weren't later." Jace shakes his head in faux disapproval. "Blake. Man. Falling down on those newlywed responsibilities."

"Judging by Hope's pink cheeks, I think he's doing just fine," Cassie says.

"Her electrical aura does seem significantly calmer," Olivia agrees, winking at Hope. "Guess I was right about the soothing power of a little love?"

Hope goes pinker. "I—you—maybe?"

"Wait, what?" I ask.

"It's simple," Olivia replies. "Lovemaking calms Hope's wiper tendencies. It puts her in balance."

"Yay! More babies!" Mom cries from the hot tub, lifting her champagne flute. She and Pop both get the giggles.

Hope laughs nervously and presses closer to my side.

And I decide I definitely need to kiss her more.

It's for her own good. Olivia said so.

"Hey, can we *not* embarrass my wife?" I ask my family.

They all exchange glances, then bust up laughing. "No," Ryan says. "Sorry, pal. Bachelor party rules dictate embarrassing you, and that means her by proximity."

"It's okay." She squeezes my hand, her eyes bright. "I like your family. They're..."

"Obnoxious?" I suggest.

"Entertaining?" Ryan says.

"Brilliant?" Cassie offers.

"Kind," Olivia interjects as she pets Chewy, who's pushed past us to get to her because the alpaca would carve *Chewpaca + Olivia 4ever* into the side of a tree if he could.

"Hilarious," Jace says over everyone else.

"*Real*," Hope concludes with a smile. "And all those other things too."

Clint opens the back door and steps onto the porch with a box full of smashed cupcakes balanced in one hand and a plate of tacos in the other, making me wonder how he opened the door at all, except he's a Marine, so I guess that's probably how.

"Eat 'em and like 'em," he says, putting the cupcakes on the table before handing me the plate of tacos.

"Ladies first." I lift a taco to Hope's lips, holding her gaze while she takes a bite.

"Oh, *yum*," she moans, and I'm suddenly wildly jealous of a taco. Only I get to make her moan like that, Mr. Taco. In fact, I want to take her home and make her moan for me all over again, even though it's barely been an hour since we made love in the kitchen.

"More?" I ask.

"*God*, yes. I'm so hungry."

While the other couples snicker—and Mom and Dad toast to more babies again—Hope takes another bite, and my cock insists that we take these tacos behind the barn and kick their asses before whisking Hope away to a place where we can be alone.

Before I can talk down my anatomy, a giant black and gray blur leaps from the roof to land smack-dab in the middle of the cupcake box, sending frosting and cake splattering everywhere as George touches down.

With matching cries of surprise, Jace and Olivia push away from the table, Jace grabbing Clover's swing in one hand and shifting it farther from the scene of the crime.

Chewpaca hums angrily at the trash panda, but he, too, backs away as George turns in a gleeful circle, greedy fingers clenching and releasing as he swims in his own private pool of cupcakes.

"George!" Ryan barks. "Get out of there!"

George defiantly shovels a paw full of icing into his mouth with one hand while he tosses Ryan half an uneaten taco with the other, a peace offering that ends up on the ground and that my brother clearly doesn't find appealing.

Or cute.

"Enough," Ryan rumbles.

"Cut it out, George!" Cassie adds as they both close in on him. "Remember the peanut butter? This will be ten times worse. Out! *Out!*"

Hope's gaze darts between the raccoon—she's helped him out of many a scrape before—and Chewpaca, who's sniffing at the taco George chucked on the ground.

"No, Chewy," I say, shifting the taco plate to one hand as I wrap my free arm around the alpaca's chest, drawing him closer as Clint gets down in George's face.

"Your superior said no cupcakes," he says, low and menacing. "Last time I checked, no means no, Private Masked Bandit."

At that, I swear the trash panda goes pale.

He drops the glob of icing in his fingers, trips over his own tail turning around, and though it takes him three tries to get his backside over the edge of the cake box, when he does, he takes off like a shot.

"Uh, thanks?" Ryan says to Clint, who straightens like he didn't just put the fear of god into our eldest brother's pet raccoon.

"He needs boot camp." Clint points at the destroyed cupcakes. "And this disaster stays in the family. No one needs to know the sins committed against dessert here tonight. Especially Cupcake."

Ryan arches a brow. "Cupcake?"

"The cupcake girl. Woman." Clint stammers, a rare crack appearing in his infamous composure before he insists in a firmer voice, "So we'll eat what's left of these, and no one breathes a word."

Ryan, Jace, and I share a look, and we all crack up all over again.

"I prefer my dessert without raccoon fur in it, thanks," I say, inspiring an "amen" from Jace and a nod from Ryan.

"Why don't we all pretend this didn't happen, and I'll go whip up a box cake inside?" Ryan turns to call over his shoulder, "Mom? You got that devil's food kind Blake loves?"

"Yep. And caramel topping and whipped cream so you can make a Better than Sex cake," she giggles before toasting us all again. "To Better than Sex cake!"

"Sounds perfect. I'll come help you!" Cassie leaps to her feet. She and Ryan lock gazes over the table, laughing softly as they pile trash into the destroyed cupcake box, sharing some private joke before they take off inside.

As the door shuts behind them, Hope sighs. "They're adorable."

"Adorably disgusting," Jace replies with a grin.

It's so weird to see him so happy, but it's good too. He's been like this since he and Olivia got married, and I'm thrilled for both of them.

Hope rubs my back and takes another taco.

"Ah, just using me for the food?" I tease.

"Yes, and sex," she murmurs for my ears only, making me chuckle.

"Texas Hold'em or five card draw?" Clint, the lone bachelor brother left, plops down at the table with a deck of cards he pulls from his back pocket. "Chewpaca. You in, dude?"

Chewy hums and nods.

Hope giggles at their interaction. "I love how normal and down-to-earth your family is."

"Al-poker!" Mom and Pop cry together, then burst into giggles, making all of us laugh too.

"Well, down to earth anyway," I say, kissing her forehead, loving that she likes my crazy family the way they are.

And me the way I am.

"Growing up must have been fun," she says, a wistful note in her voice.

"Most days. Unless Ryan was being a prick about making the rest of us do our chores, or Jace was getting in trouble, or Clint was getting struck by lightning."

She laughs, but then stops. "Wait. For real?"

Clint points to a spot on his head where his hair grows in white if he lets it get long enough. "Only patch of scared I got on me."

"So you're surrounded by electrical freaks?" she asks me.

"You're not a freak." I wrap an arm around her and kiss her head. "Clint, maybe, but not you. You're a gorgeous, sexy, big-hearted, animal-loving woman."

"It's so good to see you two together," Olivia says, twining a lock of her long blond hair dreamily around her finger. "You star charts are so compatible in the long term, but it looked like there might be a few bumps in the road early on. I'm so glad you've come through whatever your troubles were."

"Thanks," I say, because Olivia is a sweetheart without a mean bone in her body.

And because she's right.

We're not all the way there, but we're getting closer.

At least I think we are.

I glance down at my wife, but Hope isn't shooting me a *but one day we'll break their hearts* glances. She's smiling and stealing the lettuce from one of my tacos, which she slips to Chewy before he can start nibbling on Olivia's dress.

I think my bride is finally finding her *own* hope.

TWENTY-ONE

Hope

It's a miracle.

I'm at my husband's bachelor party, with electric bug lamps buzzing around the table and lights strung overhead, and not a single one of them is flickering as I stare down Clint in the final hand of the night.

Half of Ryan's Better than Sex cake, a five-dollar bill, a bottle of wine from Blake's very first crop, a roll of quarters for the arcade games at Jace's bar, and one of the raccoon babies are in the pot, though probably the raccoon baby won't actually go home with the winner, since Ryan and Cassie are both out, and none of us have any intention of breaking up George's family.

Mr. and Mrs. O'Dell went to bed tipsy an hour ago, and Olivia is leaned back in a deck chair, lightly snoring with Clover tucked into her sling and also lightly snoring.

Blake's right beside me, arm around me, whispering all

the naughty things he wants to do to me when we get home, and making Clint think he's whispering ways to cheat at poker.

I have a half-bottle of wine in me, and everything is happy.

Fun.

Perfect.

Exactly what a night with good friends should be.

Except these aren't just my friends.

They're my new *family*.

Family has always been a four-letter word to me, but the O'Dells—well, there's a reason I agreed to officiate Jace and Olivia's wedding.

I believe the two of them can make it. They're the kind of people who seem to instinctively know how to do love right.

But maybe we all possess that instinct, deep down. Maybe it's just a matter of being brave enough to trust your heart and let it lead the way.

Minnie O'Dell isn't my mother. She wouldn't have left another message today demanding answers.

She *hasn't*.

She's just accepted me.

The way I always wanted my own mother to accept me.

Blake knows how to do this right.

And with help, I know I can get there too.

"All right, civilian, show me what you've got," Clint says.

We both lay our cards on the table, and I groan. "Cheater!" I say.

Chewpaca hums in agreement behind me.

"You *always* get a royal flush," Ryan says, shaking his head. "How the hell do you do that?"

"Karma." Clint pulls the winnings his way, gently lifting the sleeping teen raccoon off the table and setting her on the porch before he jabs his fork into the cake and takes a giant bite. "Mmmmm, so gooooood." He sighs. "But is it really better than sex? I can't remember."

"Aw, Clint, are you having trouble getting laid?" Jace taunts.

"Hush your mouth," Clint slurs. "That's my private penis business."

"PPB, huh?" Ryan chuckles. "You're wasted, aren't you?"

"He had nearly a bottle of Jack. Of course he's wasted," Blake, who hasn't had a drop to drink in hours, points out.

"I've seen him do a full bottle and not show it," Jace replies.

"That wasn't jetlagged and after all day alpaca guard duty." Blake rises and holds a hand out to me. "Great bachelor party, family, but we're out of here."

"Aww, I'm so happy for you two," Cassie sighs.

She's also not drinking tonight, which no one has mentioned.

And good for her if that's a subtle clue. But though I'm warming up to the idea of being part of Blake's family, I'm not warming up to the idea of having babies anytime soon.

I need to get more comfortable with *me*, and then with *me and Blake*, first.

We lead Chewpaca back around front to my trailer, me giggling as Blake swears that Clint probably cheats, but nobody's man enough to call him on it, since he can kick all their asses at the same time with one arm tied behind his back.

He's joking, I'm sure.

Mostly.

"But I'm glad you can appreciate the insanity," he says when we're on the road.

Insanity. God, if he only knew.

"My family isn't like yours," I hear myself blurt out. If Blake and I are going to make a real go of this, he should know what he's getting into. "They're...hard."

He reaches over and squeezes my hand. "All families can be hard sometimes."

I shake my head. "Not like mine." I take a deep breath. "There won't be any nights like this. There won't be...much of anything. Not anything pleasant at any rate."

"That's okay," he says, threading his fingers through mine.

"Yeah?" My lips curve in a weak smile. "You sure? I wouldn't blame you if you wanted no part of the dysfunction. I'd gladly swap families with you if I could."

"You can have mine."

"Because you don't want them?" I laugh.

"No, because we'll share them. *Together*."

"Oh."

I fall silent, realizing that the radio display isn't flickering, and neither are the headlights or dash lights in Blake's shiny new truck. Only the hula man is wiggling.

It's been a long time since I've gone a whole day without short-circuiting something.

It's been a long time since I felt this...light.

But I want to be even lighter. I want Blake to know it all.

"That's part of the problem, I think," I whisper to the moon out the window. "I've never seen a healthy love relationship up close. My parents are miserable together."

Blake rubs his thumb over the back of my hand. "Sometimes knowing what *not* to do is its own superpower."

I let out a shaky breath. "But there are *so* many different ways to screw up. So many ways to let another person down."

"That's where forgiveness comes in. We're both gonna screw up. We're human. It's what we do. But I'd rather screw up and make up and keep fighting to make love work with you than have it easy with anyone else."

I look back at him, the backs of my eyes beginning to burn.

So many times now, he's said he loves me, and I believe him.

I do.

And I love him too. I've loved him for a long time.

I just need to find it in me to fully commit to this leap, to dive into the love lagoon and pray I miss the rocks. Because Blake deserves that kind of love, the fearless, cliff-diving kind, and I'm so tired of being afraid.

Too bad being sick of Fear isn't always enough to pry the bastard's bony fingers from around your throat.

"Let's just take it one day at a time, like we said," Blake says softly, as if he senses the war waging inside of me. "I'm not going anywhere, and I'm not in any rush."

"If every day could be like today, I'd be a very happy woman," I whisper.

He grins. "Arguments with your cousin and all?"

"Well, you were *very* heroic during the argument part. It was pretty hot."

"Yeah?" he asks, his chest puffing up, making me laugh.

"Yes. But now you look like a rooster on the verge of a victory strut."

"I'll do that when we get home," he says, wiggling his brows. "Naked. The way god intended."

I giggle again. "But seriously. Thank you. For the heroics."

"No thanks needed. Just doing what I do for the people that I love."

His words wrap around me like a warm cocoon, and I lay my head on his shoulder for the rest of the trip.

He's not my father. Nor my mother.

He's a solid man, with a crazy, loving family, and he knows how to do this *right*.

All I have to do is trust him to lead the way.

"Maybe I do need an alpha alpaca sometimes," I sigh beneath my breath.

"What's that?" Blake asks.

"Nothing," I say with a smile, because if I tell him he's my love alpha, he'll never let me live it down.

When we get back to the farm, we walk Chewpaca back to the barn together. Too-Pac isn't sleeping yet—he's waiting for his friend, and the two of them have a short conversation that makes me smile once we get Chewy back in their shared pen.

"You think he's safe tonight?" Blake asks. "I can take first watch if you think Kyle is still a threat."

"No, if there's a problem, the dogs will let us know." I hook a finger into the collar of his shirt and tug. "Besides, I have other plans for you."

He growls low in his throat. "Dirty plans, I hope?"

"Filthy," I assure him.

He puts his arms around me. "Me and you? The empty stall? Five seconds? I've always wanted a literal roll in the hay."

"Right here, where all the baby animals can hear?" I tease. "Dildo Shaggins would never suggest such a thing."

"Oh, so you think Dildo Shaggins can do for you what I

can do for you?" He bends his head, kissing my cheek, my jaw, my neck.

I shiver. "Maybe. I could head back to the house alone and give him a try."

"I don't think so, love-muffin. Not unless I can watch, and then prove which one of us is better."

"You're awfully confident," I murmur.

"Cocky, some might say."

"Very cocky." I nip at his ear before I add in a whisper, "Take me to bed, Mr. O'Dell. I want to shag you senseless."

Without another word, he scoops me up in his arms and races for the house.

And it's not because anyone's watching.

It's just because he wants me.

The same way I want him.

TWENTY-TWO

Blake

I wake up alone again, but this time I'm in Hope's bed, with early morning light slowly chasing away the shadows and revealing a note on her pillow.

Blake –

Thank you for an amazing night. I didn't want to wake you, but needed to feed the animals. Coffee's prepped and there are cinnamon rolls from the bakery on the table.

xo,

Hope

I sit up slowly and scratch my head, smiling at her handwriting while my mind wanders to the events of last night. The sexy events. And the sweet ones too.

She knows how to do this love thing.

She just doesn't *know* that she knows.

But she didn't run away. She left a note.

I'm still smiling while I throw the covers back and head

for the shower. Five minutes later, I'm pulling on clothes and heading off to help my wife.

But I don't make it all the way down the porch before I see her running down the path from the barn. Sprinting, actually.

She's definitely not out for a leisurely jog.

Something's wrong.

"Hope? What—"

"Chewpaca!" she gasps. "Blake, *he took Chewpaca!*"

"What? *Who?*" I jog down the last few steps.

"Kyle!" A sob wrenches from her chest. "He's gone. Kyle must've taken him."

"Hey. Hey." I pull her into my arms, the hairs on my arms lifting as a buzzy feeling sweeps across my skin. "We'll get him back. C'mon. I'll drive. You call the lawyer."

We hop in my truck, but when I put my key in the ignition, it shocks me hard enough to make me cry out and pull my hand away. When I try again, the engine won't turn over, and Hope hands me my phone with another ragged sob. "*I broke it.* I broke it before I could call the lawyer or the sheriff or anyone."

"Okay. New plan. We, uh... We just—"

Shit.

What *do* we do?

I can fix the truck, but it'll take time. We could take her truck, but she'll probably short out her starter too.

"Let's just think for a second." I slam out of the driver's seat and circle the truck, racking my brain, and then it hits me.

I know *exactly* how to get to Kyle's place.

Hope's still in the passenger seat, face in her hands, looking every bit as defeated as the day we ran into each other in Vegas four years ago. I pull open the truck door and reach over to unstrap her seatbelt. "It's going to be okay, Hope, we're going to get him back."

"How? Kyle has more money and better lawyers and—*mmph!*"

I press my lips to hers and thread my fingers through her hair, tasting coffee and panic, and she slowly relaxes into me and kisses me back.

Kind of.

"No—time—save—Chewpaca—*oh*," she murmurs between kisses.

"Trust me, baby," I whisper against her lips.

She melts into me, and I make love to her sweet mouth until I feel that humming, fizzing sensation prickling at my skin begin to fade away. When it's gone, I give her one last sweet kiss before I pull back and tip her chin up. "You okay?"

She blinks twice, then nods slowly. "Yeah. I'm okay. At least okay enough not to blow anything else up."

"Then let's take your truck."

We switch vehicles, and I get her old beater going without a hitch. As soon as we're flying down the road, I grip her hand. "Just breathe. It'll be okay. Feeling like you can try the lawyer on your phone?"

She nods, but keeps a firm grip on my hand while she dials Mr. Ashford.

I steer us through Happy Cat to the sprawling neighborhood not far from the golf course, where the richest residents live in mini mansions with ten-acre lots of rolling green grass, while Hope leaves a message for the attorney about custody of Chewpaca. She hangs up as I'm pulling her truck to a stop in front of the two-story brick colonial where Kyle lives. "I'm not going to call the sheriff yet. Not if we can work this out peacefully first. St. Claires don't like to make scenes." She hands the phone over. "But be ready if things turn ugly."

She's up the sidewalk and charging past the white porch columns before I'm fully out of the truck.

"Open up, Kyle! I know you're in there!" She pounds her fist on the door. "I can smell the stink of laziness and alpaca-napping from all the way out here!"

"I should've run over his rosebush," I mutter.

"It's not the rosebush's fault he's an asshole." She jams a finger into the doorbell, which issues one gargled chime before it explodes with a sharp *pop*, and a thread of smoke drifts lazily into the morning air.

"Maybe we can figure out how to channel this electrical energy for the forces of good," I say as she starts banging on the door again. "Get you a super suit or something."

"Superheroes aren't real," she grits out.

"Yes, they are. You're a superhero."

She stops banging and looks at me, pain filling her pretty brown eyes, and I want to scoop her up and take her and all of her animals away from this bullshit.

Far, far away.

Winery be damned.

I just want her to be safe and happy and loved.

"You're a superhero to every single one of those animals you rescue," I continue, answering the dubious wrinkle of her brows. "You nurse them. You give them a home. You fight for them. Even the ones no one else wants. *Especially* the ones that no one else wants. That's more heroic than anything I've done in my life, and it's inspiring. I'm so proud of you."

She blinks like she's on the verge of tears again. "I— thank you. I don't...I don't think anyone's ever said that to me before."

My head rears back. "You can't be serious."

"I'm a college dropout without a *real job*." She makes air quotes around *real job*, and I want to punch whoever made her feel like college and a paycheck from someone else is all that matters in life. "That doesn't count for pride points where I come from."

"You stand on your own two feet and save more lives in any given week than most people do in a lifetime. You're amazing. Don't let anyone ever tell you otherwise."

The door swings open, and a droopy-faced Kyle with hooded lids, wearing a rumpled suit jacket paired with a pair of bright green jogging shorts, stares stupidly at us. "Whaddya want?" he slurs.

Hope lunges for him, but I grab her before she can get her hands around his throat.

"We want the alpaca back," I tell him. "Now."

"You nasty, thieving, lying scumbag," she adds. She pauses, and then she spits at his feet. "And that's for every time you called him a llama."

His barely-focused eyes sharpen. A little. "Whadder you talkin' 'bout?" He points an unsteady finger at the ground and adds, "Thas gross. And unlady—" He burps. Loudly. Before finishing without a trace of irony. "Unladylike."

Hope grimaces and rears back with a soft gag as the scent of him drifts out onto the porch.

Dude smells like he showered in stale whiskey while chugging a six-pack of cheap beer.

"Oh my god. Are you *drunk*? At eight in the morning?" she asks.

"Where's the allapama?" He shakes his head, grabs the door frame to steady himself, and mutters, "*Whoa.*"

"If you hurt Chewpaca, *whoa* is the last thing you'll ever

say." Hope waves a hand in front of her face, presumably to disperse the stench. I hold my breath, not certain any amount of hand waving will help. "I talked to the attorney yesterday," she continues, "and he says he specifically told you *two days ago* that you needed to wait for the court date."

"Not gonna happen." He uses his forearm to wipe at his nose. "No court. No allapama jizz money. No happiness. Nothing but misery and..." He burps again. "Despair."

Hope looks up at me. "Shit. He's useless."

"She's gone. Gooooone. Gone." He grabs a forty of malt liquor from just inside the door and tips it back, then lifts it higher and shakes, squinting one eye up into the bottle.

A single drop falls out and lands in his eye. "Pain, sweet pain," he croaks in response. "And now I'll never see 'er again."

"Cara left you?" Hope asks.

"She had abraca-astigmakismata. Got new glasses yesterday. When she realized my dick was normal size, it was bye-bye Kyle Gaylord Jr."

My forehead wrinkles as questions I can't ask zip through my brain—couldn't she *feel* what size his dick was? How blind was this woman? And how am I just learning that Kyle's middle name is Gaylord? This is something he should have been tormented for the entire time he was growing up in Happy Cat, even if he was home-schooled.

"So you won't win Chewy in court," she says, voice tight with barely controlled anger. "Is that why you stole him?"

Kyle rubs his eye. "Not unless I drunk him while I was stole." He frowns. Burps. Puckers his lips. "Stole him drunk I was while." He waves a hand. "You mean what I know."

"*Then who has the alpaca, Kyle?*" she demands.

He blinks at us with one semi-clear eye, and one disinfected-by-booze eye. "Hey, yeah. Where is he? What's going on? You lost Gam-gam's prize alpaca?"

"So Chewy's really not here?" I ask, wanting to be one-hundred-percent sure before we expand our search.

He glances behind him. "I mean, we can look, but I didn't put him here."

"Damn it," Hope murmurs. "I think he's telling the truth."

"Call Cassie," I say. "Tell her to get everyone to the sanctuary. We can organize a search party there. I'll sober up Mr. Heartbreak, and meet you there as soon as I can."

"Don't wanna be sober," Kyle says, nose wrinkling.

"You'll love it," I assure him, clapping him on the back. "My brother's a bartender. Has all the best tricks to make it painless."

"What are you going to do?" Hope asks.

I grin. "Whatever's easiest."

She shoves me out of the way. "Then *I'm* sobering him up, because I've always wanted to dunk him in a bucket of water. You call the troops. I'd probably break the phone anyway."

"Remember we might need him to talk," I call as I trail her into Kyle's house, which is overflowing with evidence of a frat party gone wrong. Bottles of beer and whiskey litter the floor, half-empty pizza boxes sit open on the stairs, and for some reason a roll of toilet paper has unrolled itself across the kitchen island and left a trail of white into the living room.

I get on group text with my brothers, who all reply nearly instantaneously to let me know they're on their way to the sanctuary. Then I take a quick tour of Kyle's house to verify no evidence of alpaca exists.

When I get back to the kitchen, Hope's squaring off

with him again, but he's dripping wet and significantly more sober.

"*I don't know,*" he says, like he's exasperated. "Who in their right mind would steal an alpaca? You and I are the only two people who know he's worth anything."

"Cara knows," I correct him.

Kyle and Hope turn as one, and Kyle mutters a curse under his breath.

Hope drives a hand through her hair. "And she was at the sanctuary with us yesterday. Not for very long, but maybe long enough to make the dogs think it was okay for her to be poking around in the barn last night? I mean, it's a long shot, but definitely worth checking into."

"C'mon," I say to both of them. "We're going alpaca hunting. Kyle, buddy, you're riding in the back. No offense, but you still smell like pickled whiskey ass."

TWENTY-THREE

Hope

I'm trying desperately not to bite my nails. I'd really love to hold Blake's hand again—it helped keep me calm on the way to Kyle's house—but instead, we're separated by the drowned and drunken rat between us.

Turns out riding in the back makes him sick to his stomach, which we learned halfway to Cara's place when he wouldn't stop banging on the back glass and turning green.

"Quit poking me," Kyle hisses.

"Payback's a bitch, buddy." I poke his leg again, because it's in my space. "Quit manspreading. Just because I'm a woman doesn't mean I don't deserve legroom. Especially since this is *your fault*."

"This wouldn't have happened if you wouldn't have married an asshole to try to fight me for the beast," he snaps back.

Then he *oof*s, which I assume means Blake got him with an elbow.

"*That beast* is worth more than just his sperm, and he deserves a happy life," I retort. "You're the one who told *your* wife what he was worth."

"I didn't think she was the type to steal a horse."

"*Alpaca.* And you're the one who hired an inept private eye to *spy* on me and my husband."

Kyle grunts. "He caught you sleeping separately, didn't he?"

"How much further to Cara's house?" Blake interrupts.

"Two blocks. See that oak tree that looks like it has a big penis growing out the side? Turn there."

I smile. "Yeah, I can see where you'd be a disappointment, if that's what she's used to looking at every day."

"Go on. Laugh. You're right. I'm an idiot." He hangs his head with his hand, and if I weren't so worried about getting Chewy back before he gets hurt, I might actually feel bad for my cousin.

I get the sense he actually *liked* Cara, as much as the snootier side of the St. Claire bloodline is capable of liking anyone, anyway.

"There," he says with a weary sigh. "The little house on the big lot."

I gasp.

It's an itty-bitty pink house that looks like it was ripped right out of the Candy Land board game and plunked down in the middle of Happy Cat.

And I do mean *itty-bitty*.

"She was on one of those home shows about going tiny after her house blew up in a gas explosion," he says forlornly. "There are drawers under her bed that work the way they're supposed to instead of getting off their tracks and sitting weird. And a table that folds out of the wall." He sniffs. "She uses it as her desk too."

Blake and I make eye contact around him.

I can't believe I actually feel sorry for my cousin.

But I'll buy him a beer later.

After we rescue my alpaca.

I hop out of my truck, Blake and Kyle on my heels. But I don't even get halfway across the half-acre lot to the ten-foot-wide structure before the door opens and Cara steps out.

"I'd throw something dramatically, but I'm a minimalist and don't have anything to spare to throw," she says. "Next time, don't tell a girl your dick is bigger than your house, especially when the house is as big as yours. I thought you cared about the earth, and instead you're taking up as much space as an entire football team, however many people that is. I'm sure it's a lot."

"We're looking for the alpaca," I explain, not wanting to get sidetracked by the relationship drama.

Cara blinks. "Then shouldn't you be at your place?"

"You didn't take him?" Blake asks.

She huffs. "Of course not. I would never force a creature from his home. I know how terrible that feels. Believe me. And I don't exactly have a spare bedroom. I had to give my fish away when I moved in."

"The fish didn't die in the explosion?" I ask, a little buoyed by the news.

She shakes her head. "No, I got him after. When I was living with my parents." Her gaze shifts to Kyle, her eyes narrowing. "Also, I don't make love like a giraffe anymore. *Someone* ruined that experience for me. Forever."

"I can try harder," he tells her.

"You're a spoiled man-child who doesn't realize the dick

is the frosting on the cupcake. The only thing that could improve your cake is another seven to ten years of honest to god personal development." She crosses her arms with an eye roll. "I'm never marrying a man again before I see his sock drawer. Now go away. I have to drown my sorrows in kombucha, and I don't want an audience."

"Can I verify that you don't have our alpaca, first?" Blake asks. "Have a quick look around? And then we'll leave you to your mourning."

She flips a hand at the house. "Oh, please. Be my guest. Spread your mistrust all over my personal sanctuary. Would you like to ruin armadillos for me while you're at it?"

"They carry leprosy," I say, hating to be the bearer of bad news, but...

"Hope," Blake mutters beneath his breath.

"But they're really adorable otherwise," I add hastily. "I love their armor."

We make a quick trip around the house, verifying that Chewpaca isn't sunning himself in the backyard or lounging inside on Cara's bed.

Actually, I can't even see the bed. Maybe it's hanging from the ceiling?

These tiny houses are really something else.

"Maybe your alpaca decided to go find a bigger herd?" Cara suggests when we get back around front. "Don't they like to have five or six buddies around for socializing and things?"

"No, he didn't leave on his own." I shudder at the memory of what I found when I went to let Chewy out this morning. "Someone sawed through the padlock and left tire tracks from the barn, and Too-Pac was *very* upset." I shake my head. "But if you two didn't take him...who did?"

"How should I know?" Her shoulders bob. "I'm a

forensic statistician. If you want a private detective, hire that goofball Kyle uses. He caught you two sleeping apart, didn't he?"

"He was cheap too," Kyle says. "You could probably afford him."

"Great." Blake snags him by the collar and starts dragging him back to the truck. "Then you can call him and pay him, because this is still your fault."

"How is it my fault?" Kyle yelps.

"Because you wanted Chewpaca for all the wrong reasons," I say. "If you'd wanted him because you loved him and cared that he had a good long life, then we could've worked something out. Instead, you hired a PI to make everything worse than Gram's will made it in the first place."

"Good luck finding your llama," Cara calls after us.

"Alpaca," Blake and I call back together.

Cara laughs. "I know. I was joking. Geez...the way you're all behaving, you'd think someone had died. I'm sure whoever took the little guy will take care of him, right? Probably just wanted something to love."

I don't dignify that with a response. Cara knows Chewy is worth a lot of money. Love had nothing to do with this. It was greed. Plain and simple.

Blake pushes Kyle back to the truck while he grips my hand. "We're going to find him," he promises me.

But *how?*

Kyle doesn't have him. Cara was a long shot, and she doesn't have him.

Or one of them is lying.

Or someone else wants Chewpaca.

My eyes water again.

I'm so tired of crying.

But Chewpaca's missing, and we don't know why or how.

I don't know if he's terrified or if he's comfortable or if he's alone or if he's been stolen to be sold off on the alpaca black market. I don't know who took him.

Or *how*.

"The dogs should've barked. Even if it was someone they've met before," I say as Blake wraps one arm around me and points Kyle into the truck with his other hand. "Why didn't the dogs bark? I didn't leave the house the entire night or morning. Maud brought over the cinnamon rolls. I would've heard the dogs bark."

"We're going to find him," Blake says again.

"But what if we don't?"

"Hope. Look at me." I blink up at him, fighting to hold it together, but the fear fingers are so tight around my neck now that I can barely breathe.

"We are going to find Chewpaca. All of us. Together," he insists. "You and me? We're family. That means you have all of the O'Dells, and the rest of Happy Cat behind you. Trust me. Okay?"

"Okay." I lean in, hugging him tight.

I don't know what I did to deserve this man in my life, but I'm so, *so* grateful that he's here.

TWENTY-FOUR

Blake

I don't have a fucking clue how I'm going to find Chewpaca.

But I made my wife a promise, and I'll be damned before I let her down.

Unfortunately, after dropping Kyle off at his house to cry into half-empty pizza boxes, we arrive at the sanctuary to find my family isn't the only crew assembled.

I make eye contact with Clint, who's corralled the O'Dell contingency on the porch, separate from the pant-suit-wearing trio standing rigidly in the shade beside the farmhouse. Before I can get more than a grimace and a shrug from my brother, however, we're spotted by the suits.

"Finally. Hope, this sham comes to an end right now." An older woman who looks like Hope iced-over, dolled up, and aged thirty years marches over to us in low heels and a pale gray suit, two men on her heels. She motions to the taller, prune-faced guy with a moustache behind her—ah, must be Hope's father, he of the judgmental, 'stache—and then the shorter, red-cheeked Santa Claus look-alike. "Hope, this is our attorney, Mr. Tweedleton. He'll be drawing up the annulment paperwork."

"Charmed," Tweedleton says with a dimple-popping grin.

"Mom, you're home early." Hope's eyes go wide as she glances between her mother and the impish lawyer. "Wh-what? No. Chewpaca is missing, and we have to—"

"Get an annulment," her mother repeats with exaggerated patience, making my fists curl. *What the hell?* "It's a process by which a marriage can be declared invalid if—"

"I know what it is," Hope says, cutting her off. "But I'm not getting one. I told you in the message I left you the other day that Blake and I—"

"Are attempting to perpetrate fraud," her prune-faced father cuts in, his voice as brittle as glass crunching beneath heavy shoes. "In order to profit from your grandmother's will."

"Hold on a minute—" I start, but Hope interrupts me.

"That's not true. Our marriage is legal. Ask Judge Maplethorpe. Or look at the records in the courthouse, everything's in order."

"Marriage fraud is a very serious charge, young lady," her father continues as if she hasn't spoken a word, his thick brows forming a disapproving V above his cold blue eyes. "One that could end with a prison sentence."

"That's only if you're paying someone to marry you for citizenship," Hope says with a tight laugh. I start to speak again, but she cuts me an *I've got this* look. "And I would never do that. Obviously. I'm already a U.S. citizen."

"But the man from Atlanta you were ready to pay five

thousand dollars to marry you isn't," her mother states, her words making Hope shrink inside her clothes.

"You know about that?" Hope whispers while I flinch.

I don't like to think about her marrying someone else.

"We know about that," her mother confirms. "Frederick Boucher is Canadian and was only too eager to forward your emails to our private investigator. I imagine he'd be just as eager to hand them over to the authorities. It's a disgrace to the family. On top of everything else you've done. Or rather, *not* done."

"But I didn't know he was from Canada," Hope says, glancing Tweeledum's way. "He has an Atlanta address. And I was going to pay *him*, not the other way around. And can we please talk about this later? Chewpaca is missing, and we have to—"

"You can get another llama," her mother says with an eye roll.

"No, I can't, Mom," Hope says, "and he's not—"

"I'm afraid it might not matter what you knew, or didn't know, about Mr. Boucher," the lawyer cuts in cheerfully— too cheerfully, making me wonder if he's drunk. I would swear I'm smelling whiskey again, but that could be Kyle's stench still burned into my nostrils. "They're cracking down on marriage fraud these days. Handing out huge fines and even jail time for the people they really want to make an example of."

"But I didn't marry Frederick." Hope's forehead wrinkles in confusion, as if she, too, is having a hard time reconciling Tweedle's upbeat tone and his doom and gloom news. She reaches for me and I take her hand, giving it a firm squeeze. "I married Blake, and I didn't pay him a dime."

"That's the truth," I confirm, but my smile petrifies on my face as Mr. and Mrs. St. Claire keep their focus on

Hope, acting as if I haven't spoken at all. Jaw clenched, I direct my next statement to the lawyer. "I married Hope because I love her, and I want to spend my life with her. That's all there is to it. Now, if you'll please excuse us. We have a crisis to deal with."

"Some might say that liquor license you recently obtained is a form of payment," Tweedle says with a grimace of commiseration that's still absurdly chipper. "And also a crisis, I'd say. The fact that Hope finagled that for you so soon after the marriage looks pretty fishy. Potentially fishy enough to be deemed fraud."

"Even if that were true," I say, quickly adding, "though it's not, I was born right here in Happy Cat. My citizenship isn't affected by our marriage and neither is hers."

"True, but there are other factors to consider." Tweedle's head bobs and another whiskey-scented breeze drifts my way.

He's definitely been tippling. It would make me wonder what the men of Happy Cat are coming to, with so many of them drunk by breakfast, but if I had to work for Hope's parents I'd probably be hitting the whiskey first thing too. They're a miserable pair, both of them oozing judgment and anger so intensely I can feel it shoving at my shoulders, snarling in my stomach, making my skin itch with a discomfort so intense that if it were anyone but Hope beside me, I would have already excused myself.

But I'm not going to leave her alone with these dismal, disapproving people. The poor thing already had to spend her entire childhood at the mercy of Cranky and Crankier, she doesn't deserve another moment of pain or suffering.

"Later," I say. "Right now Chewpaca is our first priority."

"There are significant assets at stake," the lawyer continues. "It might be enough to get law enforcement involved. And with confirmation of your attempt at bribery in his back pocket, if your cousin decided to bring a civil suit against you, he'd almost inevitably win."

"Just because I tried to pay one man to marry me doesn't mean I paid Blake." Hope turns to her parents. "And no one ever would have known about Frederick if you'd trusted me. And Blake's right. *We need to find my missing alpaca.* All of this can wait."

Hope's mother makes a sound that could be a laugh or a cough. Whatever it is, it's unpleasant. "Trust that you've made an informed decision about a life partner you randomly married one morning? Please, you barely know each other."

"That's not true," Hope protests. "He knows me better than either of you ever will."

Both St. Claires snort in response to that, and my outrage bubbles over.

How can they treat her like this?

"I know her and I love her," I say, putting my arm around her shoulders and drawing her close to my side. "If the liquor license is the problem, I'll give it back. She's more important to me than opening a tasting room."

Hope's head jerks my way and her jaw drops. "No, Blake, it's your dream, I can't let you—"

"You're my dream." I gaze into her sweet face, wishing I could turn back time and rescue the little girl she was from the horrible people who raised her. But I can't take away that pain. All I can do is make sure she has a home filled with love from now on. "Nothing else is ever going to matter the way you matter."

Her eyes fill and her lips part, but before she can speak, her father cuts in.

"He's clearly after your inheritance, Hope," he sneers in a way that makes me want to punch him. Or maybe beat him with Dildo Shaggins, because I get the feeling he'd find that way more insulting than a simple punch. "Don't be a fool," he continues. "Men like this are always looking for a reason not to put in an honest day's work, and you've fallen right into his trap."

The punching-urge grows stronger, but I force my hand to remain still and loose by my side.

I will not punch my wife's father, no matter how much he deserves it. I was raised better, and if there's even the ghost of a chance we might all be able to get along, I'll do whatever it takes to make that happen.

For *her* sake, not his.

"So which is it, Dad?" Hope lets out a humorless laugh. "Am I a criminal who's so pathetic and unlovable I had to buy myself a husband? Or a fool who's fallen into a golddigger's trap? Tell me quick so I can go find my missing alpaca."

"Please, Hope, don't be so dramatic," her mother says with a disdainful sniff. "You've made a mistake, and we're here to clean up your mess before it gets any worse. Let's leave it at that."

"I won't leave it at that," Hope says, her voice thick with emotion. "And I'm not leaving Blake, not unless he asks me to. I want to make this marriage work, even though I'm scared to death I won't be good enough for him."

I hug her closer. I want to tell her that she's far too good for me. And I will, but not in front of her parents. They don't get to see any more of our private life. They've proven they don't deserve that kind of access.

Her mother's eyes narrow. "Then so be it. But don't

come to us for help when you find yourself in the middle of a legal battle you can't afford."

"Or end up losing half your inheritance to a man who married you for money," her father adds. "Because he'll want his half before he grants you a divorce, girl. You can be absolutely sure of that."

"Can I?" Hope asks, anger flickering to life in the words. "Because he didn't ask for a dime the first time we got an annulment four years ago."

I stiffen—shocked to hear her say it aloud—but when she looks up at me, I nod.

Hell yes, let's tell the truth. *Finally.* I'm tired of keeping secrets and pretending I haven't wanted to be with her for a hell of a lot longer than the past few days.

"We got married in Vegas four years ago," Hope continues, her gobsmacked parents keeping their mouths shut for once. "But we had it annulled because we were young and..." She trails off, taking a deep breath before she continues, "No. That's not the truth. We got an annulment because I was scared of marriage. But I was never scared of Blake. Not a single day in my entire life. He makes me happy." Her voice breaks, but she keeps going. "He makes me feel beautiful and special. Like I'm someone worth fighting for, and I want to make him feel the same way."

Before I can assure her that she makes me feel that and so much more, Clint shouts from the porch, "He's an ugly bastard in comparison, Hope, but he's crazy about you. We've all known it for years."

"And we're here for you guys!" Cassie calls.

"No matter how full of shit you are," Jace adds.

"This is just a bump in the road on the way to all the beauty waiting in your future," Olivia says before adding in a more plaintive voice, "and it's never too late to make a change for the better. Love is always there, just waiting for you to say yes."

The words are clearly aimed at the St. Claires, but her lovely sentiment bounces off their anger shields and falls to the ground.

"And I'm tired of wasting time on pointless discussions when we've got an animal to save," Clint adds. He's got his Marine face on now. "Either join the search or remove yourselves from the property."

The St. Claires' eyes go wide.

"He's right," Hope says softly. "I think you should leave."

"Agreed," I say from beside her, where I intend to stay for a very, very long time, no matter what her parents or anyone else has to say about it.

A chitter of what sounds like agreement sounds from the other side of the fence, where Too-Pac is grazing in the pasture, looking as forlorn as I've ever seen an animal to be without his buddy. A moment later George Cooney drops onto the grass on our side and waddles across the parking lot wearing a familiar hat. When he spots Hope's parents, he erupts in raccoon conversation again.

Her mother looks at me. Then Hope. Then the trash panda, who plops onto his back and rudely scratches his undercarriage with something silver he has clutched in one claw, a challenging gleam in his eye. She huffs in disgust, circles her hand in "let's wrap this up" gesture, and stomps off to the Acura parked beside the house, the lawyer and Hope's father following in her wake.

They don't even say goodbye.

Or toss a parting shot over their shoulders.

They're just...done with their daughter.

Just like that.

And good fucking riddance because they don't come close to deserving her.

"I can't say how this will play out in a court of law," Tweedle says in a hushed voice. "But I think you two are a darling couple." He glances furtively over his shoulder before turning back to me with an intense, grin-free expression. "Love her, son. And don't ever let her go. There's nothing soft waiting to catch her, if you get my drift."

"I do," I say with a nod. "And I won't let her go," I promise her, gazing into her tear-filled eyes, my chest squeezing tight. "Don't cry, baby. It's all going to be okay."

"It will. Oh, it most certainly will," Tweedle says, before he pauses and his eyes go wide with a snap of his fingers. "Oh, and Hope, I've been trying to call your cousin to warn him about that private investigator he hired, but he's not answering his phone. Apparently, the man was trying to extort your parents."

Hope stands up straighter and a cold rush of dread floods into my veins. "Who? Dean?" she asks.

George waddles over and plops down on my foot, now scratching his armpit with the silver square he's holding, making me think Ryan might want to check the trouble-maker for fleas.

"Yes, apparently a man named Dean Finister offered to sabotage your marriage in exchange for an exorbitant fee," Tweedle says quickly. "When your parents refused, insisting they'd hire their own investigator to look into the matter, things got ugly. Threats were made and he ran over the marble statue of your Great-Uncle Oliver on his way out." He looks over his shoulder again, to where the St. Claires are slamming into the car and firing up the engine. "I have to go or they'll leave me, but call me if you need anything. Wishing you both the best!"

"Thank you." Hopes waves numbly as Tweedle scurries away. Meanwhile, George is now scratching at my boot with the metal square, leaving thin scars on the leather. I bend down, plucking it from his fingers, and frown.

It's a business card holder.

With the name Dean Finister engraved on the front.

And it's full of business cards, his and the cards of other people he must have met in his travels.

Hope looks up at me with haunted eyes. "Are you thinking what I'm thinking?"

I pluck out a business card with an elegant-looking farm sketched across the bottom—a card for a guy who deals in alpacas. "That a man so desperate for money he'll threaten strangers might decide stealing an alpaca is an easier way to make a buck?"

She scans the card, her eyes starting to shine again. "Shit, yes. Of course! Dean's the only other person who knew Chewy was worth something. I can't believe I didn't think of him sooner. I feel so stupid."

"Don't feel stupid," I say. "I didn't think of him, either. He played it so damned nice from the beginning."

"To throw us off the scent." She bites her thumb. "What are we going to do?"

"We're on it, Hope," Cassie says, trotting off the porch. "I'm already posting a BOLO to InstaChat. Anyone have a picture of him?"

"I love it when you use words like *BOLO*," Ryan says.

Clint steps between them. "This him?" he says, holding out his phone. "Ruthie May sent me pictures from bingo."

"That's him!" Cassie replies. "Shoot it to me and I'll post that *Be On The Lookout* memo."

While they rally the town, Hope turns to me. "Are you mad at me?"

I shake my head. "No, of course not. Why would I be mad at you?"

Her lips turn down. "Because I spilled my guts about our first wedding in front of everyone."

I smile. "I don't care. And obviously they don't either." I nod toward my family on the porch. They're pretending not to be listening in while they're working, but I'm sure they're hanging on every word. "Do you guys?"

A chorus of "nope," "no way," and "are you kidding?" fills the air, but Hope's relieved grin only lasts a second before it fades away.

"And you're not mad about the terrible things my terrible parents said?"

"I won't lie, I wanted to punch your dad, but that's not your fault." I give her upper arms a squeeze. "I'm just sorry they don't treat you the way you deserve to be treated. Because you're the best and if they don't see it, they're as dumb as a box of dildos."

She laughs even as tears spill down her cheeks. "Thanks. I love you. So much."

My throat tightens, the joy that swells inside me at finally hearing those words almost more than I can take. "Me too. More than George loves cake."

"Will you marry me again when this is all over?"

"I will marry the hell out of you, baby," I promise. "As many times as you'll let me. Now let's go find my man of honor."

"Chewy would be a great man of honor," she says, not missing a beat. "But I might need him to walk me down the aisle, considering the state my father's in."

"Nonsense," a deep voice pipes up from the porch. We both turn to see my father standing at the railing, a misty look in his eyes as he adds, "I'll walk you down the aisle, sweetheart. It would be my honor to help welcome you to the family."

"Your forever family," my mom adds firmly, making Hope burst into tears.

But they're happy tears. I know because the same damned thing is happening to my face. I'm a fucking mess, but it's okay. I've got the best family in the world, and if anyone can find a lost alpaca with nothing but a business card to go on, it's these hard-loving, zero-shit-taking people.

Hope makes the call to the sheriff's office, and within four minutes, Cassie has a lead. "Someone posted on Insta-Chat that they spotted a vintage Ford station wagon with a white alpaca leaning its head out the window headed out of town on the highway to Atlanta!"

"Oo-rah!" Clint yells.

"I'm calling the sheriff," Ryan says.

"The dogs!" Hope suddenly shrieks. "I need to let the dogs out to run. And the goats need to be fed and milked, and—"

"We've got them," Olivia tells her, and Jace nods. "You go get my favorite alpaca back."

We pile into Hope's truck, and Clint and Ryan hop into Ryan's truck to follow us, and we're off, on our way to bring Chewy home. Because, in the immortal words of the blue alien from that movie I loved as a kid, family means no one is left behind.

TWENTY-FIVE

Blake

The sheriff tells us all to sit tight and wait for the deputies to report back with news.

We, of course, pay zero attention to that and divide ourselves into search parties.

Forget waiting for the sheriff's deputies.

We have an alpaca to save.

Hope and I are racing down the highway, me driving, while she stays plugged in to InstaChat for alpaca-spotting updates, while Ryan and Clint follow a short distance behind.

"I thought he was one of the good guys," she fumes, refreshing the screen for the hundredth time. I keep waiting for a sign that she's going to go uber-electric and short it out, but nothing's buzzing despite her clear anger with Dean. *"People who do yoga in the grass beside a field shouldn't steal animals.* He should know that's terrible karma."

I reach over and take her hand. "He won't get away with it."

She bites her lip and nods. "No, he won't." Dropping her cell into her lap, she brings both of her hands to cradle mine. "And Blake...I meant what I said to my parents. I love you. I've loved you for a long time. I'm sorry I've been too weird to say it."

"Ah, baby, I know. You *show* it. Even when you don't mean to." I squeeze her fingers. "And I like you weird. Don't ever change."

She smiles. "Couldn't if I tried, so that works out." Her phone dings, and she releases my hand to grab it, getting an update that has her bouncing in her seat. "Turn right!" she says, pointing to the exit up ahead. "Lizzie at the Kennedy Family Day School just spotted them heading toward the river port a few minutes ago! She said Chewpaca looked angry, but wasn't trying to climb out the window."

I swing a hard right onto the exit that quickly becomes a graying county road that'll take us the short way to the river dock.

"Blake?" Hope says, gripping my thigh through my jeans like a lifeline.

"Yeah?"

"Thank you so much. For being here and...everything else."

It kills me that she feels the need to thank me for being a decent human being, and that she didn't have the love or support every kid needs growing up. But it means the world that she's opening up and letting me into her thoughts.

And into her heart...

"*Anything* for you," I say. "Anything."

She leans in, pressing a quick kiss to my cheek that warms me all the way to my core before she hops on the phone to call Ryan and tell him the latest. "Okay, sounds good," she says after she gives him the update. She nods my way as she points straight ahead. "You guys head to the north boat ramp and we'll take the south. Touch base soon."

I push the pedal closer to the floorboard, racing past the first entrance to the river port toward the second nearly a mile away. Since the Army Corps of Engineers shifted the locks on the Chattahoochee to an appointment-only basis, this port doesn't get nearly as much action as it did in the heyday of the big river barges. But there are still an abundance of smaller boats that don't need the locks to ferry people and product up and down the river, and farmers who prefer to move their crops and animals via water.

Hopefully one of them isn't loading up a stolen alpaca right now...

We're almost to the south entrance when Hope's phone dings again.

"It's Olivia," she says. "Dean must have tossed the dogs steaks to keep them from barking. She found T-bone remnants in the kennels. What a bastard!"

"You don't like the dogs to have steak?"

"Yes, but only I'm allowed to give it to them so they like me best. Oh! Blake! Look!"

She points through the trees as they open up to reveal the riverfront and largely abandoned docks. A lone tugboat is rumbling at the end of the closest pier, and *there he is* —Dean dragging a clearly reluctant Chewy up onto the boat and tying him to the railing.

We careen around the last corner and I pull right up to the edge of the pavement before slamming on the brakes, holding a hand out to protect Hope, even though she's in her seatbelt, until the truck's fully stopped.

And then we're both flying out of the cab.

"Dean Finister, unhand my alpaca!" she shouts.

Chewy shrieks in what sounds like a mixture of terror and excitement to hear his mama's voice, and Dean whirls around, bracing himself on the railing, which whines audibly under his weight. God only knows where he dug up this boat, but it looks about two hundred years old, with peeling blue and gray paint, a window broken out of the wheelhouse, and black smoke belching from the top pipe.

Chewpaca wails again and strains at his lead, but the creaking railing where he's tied holds. For now.

"S*top!*" I order as I race onto the pier, Hope on my heels.

"Stay back, or I'll toss him in the river!" Dean lifts both hands into the air. "I'm sorry to do this to you nice folks. It's not personal, but I need the cash."

"You were *a cop!*" Hope cries.

"Cops have gambling debts too, honey, and I'd like to live to see my next birthday." He kicks the plank off the boat, and it starts to list away from the dock before we've reached it.

"We trusted you," Hope sobs. "Blake!"

"He's not getting away!" I assure her. I'm close enough.

I can make it.

Sprinting hard across the last few yards of the pier, I take a flying leap, soaring across open water for a heart-skipping moment before I roll onto the deck of the boat.

The wood planks let out an ominous groan and one board snaps in half beneath my knee as I rise to my feet.

Fuck.

How old *is* this thing?

I start toward Dean, but am frozen in my tracks by a war cry sailing through the air behind me. A beat later, Hope lands next to me with a thump before tumbling onto her hands and knees.

"You okay?"

"Just fine," she assures me, clinging to my arm as I help her up. Her eyes narrow as they fix on Dean, who's untied Chewy and is dragging him in the other direction. "Push that animal overboard, and you're heading over next."

"How about you let me borrow him for a few months," Dean bargains, grip tightening on the lead. "You've got plenty to keep you busy."

"You're scaring him, stop it," Hope insists as we advance on the older man and the clearly distressed animal, who's prancing in place while emitting a warbling, bird-like cry.

"It's over, Dean," I growl. "Hand over the alpaca and take us back to shore, and the authorities will go easy on you."

I have no idea if that's true, but the truth comes second to getting Hope and Chewy safely back on dry land before this death trap falls apart in the water.

"Get off my boat!" Dean pushes Chewy into the wheel-house. "You're trespassing on private property!" He slams the door shut behind him.

Hope props her hands on her hips and shouts at Dean through the shattered window. "And *you* came onto my private property and stole my friend, you asshole. I can't believe I felt sorry for you! I almost brought you coffee!"

I grab the wheelhouse door handle and tug, only for it to come off in my hand. I curse, but a broken handle won't stop me. "Open up." I pound my fist on the door, which rattles loosely in its frame. "Last chance, before I come in there and throttle you with my bare hands."

Dean makes an "ah ah ah" sound and warns me to

"watch that temper, son," and I put my boot through the door, which is crazy easy to do.

Shouldn't this thing be made of metal?

I kick the door again, higher this time, and it swings open, revealing a wheelhouse in even worse shape than the rest of the boat, complete with rotted floorboards on one side and an insane number of rabbit feet dangling from the wheel. The fact that whoever hung them thought superstition was a viable option for keeping the vessel seaworthy makes me even more eager to get the people and animals I love *off* of it.

Chewpaca groans, his eyes wide in his head as he strains against the rope, but Dean only clings tighter to his captive. He backs into the far corner of the space, summoning a yelp of pain from Chewy as he shoves him against a rusty filing cabinet just barely secured to the wall.

"Let him go!" Hope shouts. "If you hurt him, I swear to god..."

A surge of electricity, like a lightning bolt gathering in the air, makes the hairs on my arms stand on end. A second later something on the control board pops and sizzles.

I reach out to Hope on instinct, but when my fingertips connect with her elbow sparks dance between us, like under a wool blanket in the winter with all the lights off. It doesn't hurt, but it doesn't feel great, either, so I pull my hand away.

"Chewy isn't a commodity," she seethes. "He's a sweet, innocent animal who deserves love and safety and as much freedom from pain as I can give him. I made a promise to protect him the day he came to live at my farm, and I intend to keep it."

There's another pop, and smoke begins to wisp from the radio.

Dean's eyes go wide.

"Hand me his lead," she demands. "Now." More sparks and a moment later smoke seeps from between the damaged floorboards on the other side of the room.

"I'd listen to her, Dean," I warn. "She's not here to play with you. Not even a little bit."

"I'm not," Hope assures him in a low, husky voice that makes me want to kiss her.

Damn, she's sexy when she's fighting for the things she loves.

Chewy tries to lunge around Dean, but he wraps an arm around the alpaca's neck, holding tight as he stares Hope down. "I'm not playing either, little girl. I've got some bad men after me, and my life matters more than some dumb animal's."

"He's not dumb," she says, hands balling into fists at her sides. "And you don't get to decide which lives matter and which don't."

"And you don't get to decide—"

"Hand him over!' she shouts.

"Get the hell off my boat, you crazy bi—" Dean's words end in a yelp as Hope jabs him with a trembling finger.

"Let. My. Alpaca. Go," she growls.

He rears back, but there's nowhere to go, and instead, he bangs his head on the corner of the filing cabinet. "Ow!"

Blood gushes from his head as a series of mini-explosions on the boat's control board sends an acrid smell through the room, and I conclude that letting Hope loose might not have been the smartest move.

Not while we're on a boat over water, anyway.

"Hope. We need to go." I ease past her, making meaningful eye contact with Dean as I mutter, "Hand him over, okay, man? Before we're all in a watery grave at the bottom of the Chattahoochee?"

After a moment's hesitation, he slowly releases Chewy, who dashes straight to Hope, licking her face and humming in relief as she hugs his neck.

"Oh, baby," she coos into his fur. "I've missed you too. Everything's going to be okay. I promise."

"No time for snuggles, folks," a familiar voice booms from the doorway. Suddenly a dripping wet Clint is at my side. "Get Hope and the llama off the boat. Stat."

"*He's not a llama!*" Hope says indignantly for at least the hundredth time.

Clint grins as more sparks sizzle from the control board. "I know. Just wanted to test a theory. Now get. This death-trap is off-limits to civilians and non-criminals. Even of the superhero variety."

"I'm n-not a superhero," she stammers.

Clint and I both look pointedly at the smoke oozing from several corners of the room.

"That was an accident," she says sheepishly. "Mostly..."

"And I'm mostly ready to get out of here." I hook an arm around her as Clint stalks toward the rapidly shrinking Dean, who's cowering into himself and covering his blood-spattered head.

I don't know what my brother's going to do to the man, and I don't care.

I just need to get Hope and Chewpaca off this boat.

Unfortunately, as we hustle outside the wheelhouse with Chewpaca humming along beside us, it becomes clear that we're too far from shore to leap back onto dry land, and the current is carrying us swiftly downstream.

"Can he swim?" I ask, studying the churning surface of the water, not liking the looks of the current.

"I think so. If he has to, but isn't there another way?"

The river isn't wide—but it's still a river, and it would be easy for both Chewy and the pair of us to get into trouble. We could wait and hope we drift closer to shore, but the smells coming from the wheelhouse behind us are ominous.

As is the smoke.

"Is there a lifeboat, maybe?" Hope dashes around the edge of the tugboat, inspecting the boxes and looking over the edges while Chewpaca trots along behind her, clearly unwilling to let his savior out of his sight.

I spot a rope, but I'm not exactly the cowboy type who can lasso a tree and pull us to shore. Which means we need to steer this boat.

I head back into the wheelhouse, but before I make it through the door, Clint strides out in a puff of smoke.

"Boat's on fire," he says. "Faulty wiring. Gotta get off. Now."

He's dragging Dean, who looks like he's had the fear of god, the devil, and my aunt Marlene put in him, which is only funny if you know Marlene. She's sweet as pie until you insult her fried okra, and then watch the hell out.

Ryan and Jace still won't go to her house alone.

"Agreed," I say. "But we need to get closer to shore first. We're not sure how Chewy is going to do in the water. Can you steer this thing?"

He shoves Dean at me. "Of course I can. Hold this criminal."

Hope gasps as Clint heads back into the smoking wheelhouse. "No! Clint, come back." She grabs my arm. "He's going to pass out from smoke inhalation."

"He won't," I assure her. "Marines don't pass out. It's biologically impossible."

"That's ridiculous. We have to get him out of there, and we have to jump," she says. "If the boat explodes, it won't matter that I love you and we saved Chewpaca because we'll all be dead!"

"She's got a point," Dean says.

"Shut it." I cut a hard look his way. "We're going to be fine."

"Not if we're dead," Dean says.

Chewpaca's ears go back, and he spits at Dean.

"Good boy," Hope says. "Now let's see about—"

The boat changes direction suddenly. I bend my knees and widen my stance to maintain my footing, then look to Hope to see if she needs help. My gaze has just connected with hers when pain explodes in my left temple.

She screams.

Dean shouts something about every man for himself.

And while the world spins, he knocks into me from behind, pushing me off the boat.

TWENTY-SIX

Hope

"Oh my god, you *killed my husband!*"

I don't think, I just charge Dean like a possessed woman, hand outstretched like I can fling lightning, which is ridiculous.

I might've been pissed enough in the wheelhouse that I could feel the static in my hair, but I'm not a freaking mutant superhero.

Even though I'm fairly certain I'm going to kill Dean for killing Blake.

"Wait, wait! I'm just trying to stay alive." Dean holds up his hands and dodges, trips over a rope, and also falls off the side of the boat.

"For god's sake," Clint grunts behind me, "now I have to save *two* of them. Walk off the boat when it hits the shore in a minute, okay? And fucking *stay there.*"

But he grins and winks at me as he flies over the side of the boat, splashing into the water like this is all a game.

Except it's not a game.

Dean could have knocked Blake unconscious.

And then he tossed him in the river.

"He could be drowning right now," I sob to Chewpaca, who rubs his face against my shoulder and hums comfortingly, like he's assuring me that Blake's still awake and pulling hard toward shore.

But the water is choppy and I can't see anything except waves and finally Clint's head popping back above the surface. "Please, please," I pray, heart racing with fear.

There's a sudden jolt under our feet, and I spin to see we've run into the shore. When I turn back to the water, Clint is still swimming.

But now he's also dragging someone behind him.

"*Ohmygod.*" My hands fly to cover my mouth.

It's Blake.

A barely moving Blake who might need CPR the moment Clint pulls him onto the shore. I have to get to him. Now.

There's a crack under my feet, furthering the urge to hurry. "Chewy! Off the boat! Come on, baby." I lead the way down over the side, reaching back to help Chewy down onto the riverbank with tears streaming down my face.

I can't stop them.

I just found my way back to Blake again.

I just told him the truth, told him how much I loved him.

And now he might be dead.

"Don't be dead," I sob as I race with Chewpaca through the bushes and bramble at the edge of the river toward where Clint is dragging Blake over the rocky riverbed. "Don't be dead."

"He's fine. Just a flesh wound," Clint says. "Better call 9-1-1 though."

Without another word, he dives back into the river.

I drop to my knees next to Blake on the sandy part of the shore. He groans and puts a hand to his bleeding eyebrow. "Christ, that asshole has a hard head," he says.

He's dripping wet, his hair in his eyes and mixing with the blood still gushing out his wound, and he's beautiful. Beautiful and alive, thank god.

I throw myself on him and hold tight.

"Hope," he murmurs. "Baby. It's all right. Shh. Don't cry."

"You're okay," I gasp.

In those few minutes when I feared the worst, my entire life had flashed before my eyes.

Lying awake in my sterile bedroom in my childhood home, more afraid to tell my parents that I'd wet the bed than I was of dragging a load of laundry down to the scary basement in the dark when I was just five years old.

My mother's disappointment when I proved to be hopeless at ballet and violin and every lesson she dragged me to in the years before she gave up on drilling the tomboy out of her only daughter.

My father's cool disapproval when I didn't finish in the top ten of my graduating class.

Their utter frustration when they had to have the air conditioner repaired—*again*—when I got too close to it while playing in the yard.

Having to tell them both that I'd flunked out of vet school because I cried so hard when one of the pets I was caring for died that I burned out an entire row of computers in the lab.

Marrying Blake.

Divorcing Blake.

Coming home, and being forced to see him every day and fighting with him all the time because anger was the only way to keep the love from spilling over into my eyes, my voice, my touch.

Marrying him again. Kissing him in the courtroom.

Making love to my husband, this incredible man who's taught me it's safe to let down my walls.

I'm not done making love to him, not by a long shot.

In all ways that a person can make love—body, heart, and soul.

"Shh," he says again, stroking my hair. "It's okay. We got Chewpaca. Dean's going down. Everything's fine."

"I just love you so much," I sob. "I still have so much to learn about *how* to love you, but I love you. You're my everything. Please don't die."

"I'm okay. I promise." His arms tighten around me, a solid reassurance that he's going to be fine, that he *is* fine, and I need to pull myself together and call for help. But where is my cell phone? And why can't I quit crying?

"Sorry," I say, sobbing harder.

"Don't be sorry. Let it out. Let it all out, Hope. You don't have to hold it in."

And for the first time in my life, I do.

I let it all out.

All the frustration and fear and regret. It all rolls out of me while I hug the man I love, the man I trust, the man I'd do anything for, no matter what.

And while I cry, the pent-up energy that seems to follow me everywhere slowly leaks out too, until I'm a bone-weary mass of uselessness catching my breath on a river-bank while Blake strokes my back and whispers that he loves me, that we're okay, that I'm okay, and that he'll always be here for me and my animals.

Finally, I force myself to sit up and inspect his injury. But I've barely had time to see that the blood seems to be slowing when something crashes through the woods next to us.

"There you three are," Ryan says, emerging from the underbrush onto the riverbank, where Chewy is calmly grazing on the tender green grass poking up from between the rocks. He squints across the river and grins. "And I see Clint has everything else in hand."

On the opposite riverbank, Clint's sitting on Dean while three sheriff's deputies hack their way through the weeds to reach them.

Blake pushes into a seated position with a groan, but Ryan and I quickly ease him back again. "Lie down," I say. "And don't move until we know it's safe."

"You gonna live, little brother?" Ryan asks.

Blake lifts a middle finger while his lips hitch up.

Ryan grins. "Yep, gonna be just fine. Paramedics are on their way though."

"Oh good, but how did you know where we—" I start, but Ryan cuts me off with a nod behind me.

The boat.

Holy crap.

It's drifted back into the river, in flames, and is sinking while smoke plumes billow from the carnage.

"Just followed the smoke," he says. "After calling for backup, because I'm not a moron who rushes into things without thinking first."

Blake flips him off again.

And then Chewy leans over and licks him.

And we all laugh and the last of the fear gripping my chest fades away. Blake's right, we're going to be okay. Better than okay.

We're going to be a family.

The best family we can be.

TWENTY-SEVEN

Blake

By the time we get back to Hope's house a few hours later, my head is still throbbing, but my heart is happy and full.

Chewpaca is safe.

Hope is safe.

And I'm *home*.

We're all home. Together.

Hope and Chewpaca and *all* the animals and me.

She ushers me straight to the bedroom, and I smile, because I love this bedroom. The happy sunshine coming in through the breezy curtains. The soft quilt on the four-poster bed that looks like someone's grandma made it, even though I know Hope's grandma wouldn't have, but still, it *feels* like love went into it. The romance novels on the night-stand. The way her limited jewelry scattered on her dresser looks like it's arranged in a smiley face.

Yep.

I love this bedroom.

And that's not the painkillers talking.

It's because this is *Hope*'s room, and I'm welcome here.

"I'm going to make sure the animals are okay, and I will be *right back* to pamper you and take care of you, understand?" she says as she makes me sit on the bed and bends to pull my wet boots off.

My clothes have mostly dried, but my boots—those are probably shot.

That's okay.

Boots are easy to replace, unlike one-in-a-million alpacas and one of a kind women like my wife.

"I'll come help you," I say, trying to rise from the bed only for her to put her hands firmly on my shoulders.

"Barefoot?" She arches a brow. "I don't think so, pooky. Leave this room, and I'll give you a matching injury on your other eye with Dildo Shaggins."

I grin. "I love you, snookums."

Her beautiful brown eyes soften, and that sweet smile shoots an arrow of happiness straight through my heart to my soul. "I love you too. I'll be back in five minutes, okay? Lie down. Rest."

I want to argue, but my head *does* hurt.

Who knew Dean was master of the head-butt?

Now he's master of the orange jumpsuit.

I almost giggle, but I don't, because that would be unmanly and I'm not that delirious yet.

Still, it's good to know we helped put a thief behind bars. The sheriff found evidence that he's been involved in a string of robberies all across Georgia, and all of his private eye credentials were falsified.

I'll be talking to Kyle about his shit taste in PI's later.

And then I'm going to talk to Hope about taking her clothes off and snuggling me naked.

That would make my head feel better.

It's the last thought I have before the sun is suddenly slanting low through the windows.

I wake up disoriented, my head not throbbing quite as much, with a warm body curled up next to me. I gingerly touch soft hair and smooth skin, and Hope squeezes me tighter.

"You're awake?"

I pet her hair again. "Good girl. Good beta alpaca."

She goes stiff.

I try—and fail—to squelch a low chuckle.

"You—you—" she sputters, but I can hear the smile in her voice.

"Ah-ah, Mrs. O'Dell. Five nice things about me, remember?"

She doesn't speak. Instead, she pushes up just far enough to lean her face in to mine and press a soft kiss to my lips. "One," she whispers.

"That was very nice," I agree.

"How's your head?"

"Better."

"Good." She sits up, and I get a better look at my wife while she slides off the bed. She's only wearing a tee shirt and underwear—which is fabulous—but she could, *and should*, be wearing fewer clothes.

And soon will be if I have anything to say about it.

I push up on my elbows. "Wait a second. Where are you —" I start, but then stop as she turns to face me, peeling her tee shirt off to reveal a white bra cradling her sweet breasts.

My lips part. My tongue goes dry.

And then my wife reaches for the waist of her panties.

My body flushes hot, and all my blood rushes below my belt.

"I love you," she says, her lips curving.

"That's definitely two good things." I can't keep the huskiness from my voice while I watch her work the simple white panties lower on her hips.

"And I don't want to hide from you ever again."

I lift my gaze to meet her soft, vulnerable brown eyes.

"I want to give you my body," she continues while she steps out of her underwear, "but that's just the beginning. I want to share everything with you, husband. The good and the bad. The happy and the sad. The ups and the downs and everything in between."

She reaches behind her back and unhooks her bra, stealing the breath from my lungs. "But most importantly, I want to share my heart, the one thing I've never dared to do with anyone else. Because no one else has ever deserved it the way you do. No one else has ever made me *believe* in it, in myself, the way you do."

"Hope," I whisper.

"You make me feel so loved. And not because I'm perfect. But because I'm perfect for you, just the way I am." She slides the bra down her arms and tosses it to the ground, revealing my brave, beautiful wife.

"I want to do the same for you," she says. "I want you to know you're always safe. And loved. And treasured. Always." She crawls back onto the bed, straddling my body. "Tell me when it hurts, and I'll stop."

"Don't ever stop."

I thread my fingers through her soft hair while she leans forward to kiss me again, her hands pushing up my shirt and setting my skin on fire. I want to stroke her everywhere, memorize every inch of her.

"Shh," she whispers while she helps me out of my shirt. "My turn. Let me take care of you."

And she does.

She strips me carefully out of my clothes. She kisses me slow and deep. She runs her hands over my body so thoroughly, I wonder if she's checking to make sure I'm all here, or if she's trying to memorize me the way I want to memorize her.

And when she takes me inside her, I know she's holding nothing back.

No more secrets.

No more hesitation.

She's all in.

I'm all in.

And this is where we're finally supposed to be.

She tries to keep things slow, gentle, but I want her so badly. Within minutes, we're both slick with sweat and I'm so close to coming, but I want—I *need* to feel her come for me first.

"Oh, god, Blake," she gasps. "I love you. *I love you.*"

It sends me over the edge. "I love you," I moan as the first tremors of her orgasm squeeze me tighter, and it's not about sex or getting off.

It's about being one with the woman that I was born to spend my life with.

Finally.

And forever.

EPILOGUE

Blake
Later That Year...

It's the happiest day of my life.

Again.

Hope is giggling, beaming, shining as she hurries through the door of Jace's bar, the Wild Hog, flanked by Cassie and Olivia, who are acting as unofficial bridesmaids for our most unorthodox wedding yet.

I can't wait to say "I do" for the third time in front of family and friends and let the whole world know this marriage is going to stick. For good.

Forever.

And this time I get to get married with my entire family present, including Clint, who's finally back home for the foreseeable future. He's been transferred stateside for an assignment nearby and it looks like we'll have him home for a nice long stretch.

It's a good time to be an O'Dell, no doubt about it, and there are days when I get worn the hell out just counting my blessings.

Like today.

Half the town of Happy Cat is crammed into the bar.

I'm flanked by my brothers and my parents, who, as Hope reaches me in front of the jukebox, close in for a group hug.

Hope decided she didn't need anyone to walk her down the aisle, after all, but she and my dad get closer every day. They're fishing buddies, who head down to the river almost every pretty Sunday evening to cast their lines, drink a few beers, and gossip about what hell-raisers my brothers and I were when we were little.

She always asks me to come along, but I always say no. She needs solo time with a loving parental figure, and I need to cook her a kick-ass dinner while she's gone. Because wooing my wife is my favorite hobby as well as my mission on earth.

"Let's get married every day," Hope murmurs into my ear.

"Sounds like a plan," I agree, taking her hands with a grin as my family steps away to take their places and wrangle the furry members of the wedding party.

Chewpaca, George and his family, and Jace and Olivia's hedgehogs—Princess and Duchess—have been given special permission from the health department to attend tonight's gathering. And they're all in fine, wedding day form. Chewpaca is dashing in a paisley scarf and straw hat with holes cut for his ears. The hedgehogs wear tiny flower crowns in their spikes, George wears his formal bow tie, and his main squeeze, Sticky Fingers, rocks a big red bow tied around the base of her tail that George clearly finds nearly as mesmerizing as his lady's generous backside.

He's a butt man, our George, a condition I can completely identify with.

I lean back, taking a discreet peek at my wife in her jeans. She's wearing the tight pair that drives me crazy, boots, and a heavier, winter-friendly buttonless blouse that reminds me of that night in the tasting room, when I finally dared to think she might be mine for real someday.

And now, here we are, and I couldn't be happier. I honestly didn't know happiness like this was possible until I found my way back to her.

"Are you checking out my ass?" she murmurs, as Ruthie May, the town gossip and the officiate of our Friends and Family Wedding takes her place in front of us.

"Guilty," I confess, slipping my arms around my bride and bending her back for a kiss so steamy soon half the bar is hooting their encouragement.

"Whoa there, mister, save it for after the vows," Ruthie May chides with a laugh. "Young folks today, always wanting to eat dessert first."

"Speaking of dessert, the cupcakes ain't here," Gerald calls from over by the bar. "Want me to run back to the bakery and grab some of the leftover muffin tops from this morning?"

"No, thank you, Gerald," Hope says. "I'm sure she'll get here eventually."

"If not, I've got an incredible vegan no-bake cake recipe. Wouldn't take me but twenty minutes to throw it together," Star calls out from one of the hammocks we've hung around the room, wanting our guests to feel relaxed and at home.

Though maybe not this at home...

"Y'all hush now," Ruthie May says. "You're sweet, but

you're chattin' when I'm supposed to be marryin'.'" A wave of laughter sweeps through the room in response and Ruthie May grins. "Good, then let's get started." She slips a quarter in the jukebox, and a second later, the first raunchy notes of "Honky Tonk Badonkadonk" rumble from the speakers. Immediately, the visor club of naughty bingo fame starts to sing along, Ruthie May shushes them, and Hope cracks up.

Because that definitely isn't one of the songs on our approved "getting hitched" list.

"Shoot," Ruthie May says, her brow furrowing as she runs a hand through her salt and pepper hair. "I thought I hit the Elvis song." She sighs. "Oh, well. Should we just go with it?"

Hope and I exchange a glance and nod at the same time. "Let's do it," I say, not caring what song I marry this woman to, as long as I get to promise her the rest of my life in front of our nearest and dearest.

"Dearly beloved," Ruthie May says, "we're fixin' to finally get these two lovebirds hitched up the right way. Blake. Hope. Put your hand on the monthly Sunshine Toys subscription box and repeat after me."

She holds out a pink and white box with a bright yellow winking sun on the top, and Hope starts giggling again.

"Ruthie May," Cassie, who is massively pregnant and about to give birth any second now, calls out from the booth where she, Ryan, and the Cooney family are sharing a large bowl of popcorn in hopes of keeping the critters out of the cupcakes if they ever arrive, "that's for swearing someone in to the board of directors at the factory, not for conducting a wedding."

"Well, they can't keep what's inside if they don't say

their vows on the box." Ruthie May lifts her nose with a sniff. "And you *know* they loved their prize from bingo."

Hope and I lock eyes, grin like the shameless Dildo Shaggins-loving people we are and as one, each put a hand on the box.

"There. That's better," Ruthie May says. "Now. As I was saying, marriage is a time-honored tradition of vowing to love one person and only one person for the rest of your life. And it's hard sometimes, and it's ugly sometimes, and sometimes you need a shot of tequila or a punching bag to get through the day." She sighs. "And the nights. Sometimes the nights can be even worse. What with nothing to do except lie there and think about all the mistakes you've made, the things you might have done differently, and the chances that passed you by while you were busy doing other things." A bittersweet smile curves her lips. "It all goes by so fast. You've gotta make every second count. Take the morning off. Make pancakes. Have seconds. Leave the dirty dishes in the sink."

She trails off and the room grows uncomfortably silent, the awkward moment broken only by a coughing fit from Gerald and an orgling sound from Chewpaca who, as usual, has found his way to Olivia's side. If his crush is in a room, it's a fair bet he'll soon be beside her.

I glance his way to see him nuzzling Olivia's neck and the blonde nodding seriously. "Of course," she murmurs to our fluffy best man before lifting a hand to Ruthie May. "Um, excuse me, but might I take over, please?" Olivia glides in, touching Ruthie May on the arm. Clover, who's very mobile now, is riding on Olivia's back in some sort of silk scarf contraption, chewing on an apple slice, while Jace wears a matching sling with the two hedgehogs tucked inside.

I'd call him whipped, except I'm the guy currently hunting for three more alpacas to round out Chewpaca's herd. I might also be the guy looking for matching name-plates for their pens in the stable and a specially-decorated drinking trough.

"I have a few things to say," Olivia continues, making the baby giggle happily, because apparently she likes her mama having things to say. "And Hope did such a lovely job with my wedding it seems a shame not to return the favor."

Ruthie May blinks like she's coming out of a trance and swipes at her shining eyes. "That's a lovely idea. I didn't realize I'd get so emotional."

"A lot of big feelings on a day like today," Olivia says kindly as she steps into Ruthie May's place and our original officiate is welcomed at the visor lady table, given a beer, and complimented on her words of wisdom for the young couple. Which seems to encourage some of the drunker visor-wearing grannies to shout out their own advice.

"And don't go to bed angry!" one calls out.

"Or forget birthdays and anniversaries," another shouts.

"Or put being right over being sweet," a third barks. "You're going to win more honey with sugar than from pouring salt in a wound and calling it medicine."

Hope and I are exchanging covertly confused looks when Gerald calls out for Olivia to, "Get this thing started already. The game's starting in an hour and at this rate we'll still be sitting here waiting for the honoring and cherishing."

"Gerald, for the love of muffin tops, just shut it and be patient," Maud calls out from the other side of the bar just as the front door bangs open, and the cupcake lady races in, a pack of apparently feral kittens at her heels.

"Sorry, sorry!" she cries, holding the white cupcake box over her head as the cats lunge at her bare legs, mewling and hissing as they take turns trying to jump up and snag their claws into her red-and-white checkered skirt. "I tried to keep them outside, but they chased me in."

Clint springs into action, leaping over tables and executing a fancy roll across the scarred floorboards before popping back to his feet to collect the cupcake box in one hand while he sweeps the cupcake lady off her feet and sets her atop a table, safely out of the way of the kittens.

"I knew I should have brought a few kennels," Hope mutters as her eyes narrow on the wild felines streaming into the bar. "Just in case."

"Always good to have a few spare kennels around on your wedding day," I agree dryly.

Her lips quirk as she lifts her eyes to mine. "I attract strays, O'Dell, you know this about me."

"I do," I whisper, for her ears only. "And you're so good with them. And with me. I love you so much."

"With every piece of my heart," she vows as George's kiddos, now full-fledged grown raccoons themselves, erupt in chitters and dive from their booth, all of them dashing over to play with the kittens—and then run away from the kittens, as the bloodthirsty pack proves too much for the coddled pet raccoons to handle.

"Dearest friends," Olivia says over the chaos, "we're gathered here today to celebrate love, the very best thing on earth. I'm so happy for you both. May you guard each other's hearts well and always shine as brightly for each other as you do today." She smiles. "Do you take each other in pandemonium and astrological storms, in sickness and in boat explosions, and everything in between?"

"We do," we say together.

"Then by the power vested in me by stardust and sunshine, I now pronounce you married in the eyes of all of the people who love you most. Now, shall we go rescue some kittens?"

"We shall." We head, hand-in-hand, to corral a few cats, protect our cupcakes from George, who is once again trying to sneak into our white bakery box, and spy on Clint and the cupcake lady, who are making eyes at each other. As usual, we laugh the entire time.

"You think every day will be like this?" I ask as we make our way to the floor to have our first dance to "Afternoon Delight," a mortifying selection that was apparently my mother's doing, since she's the only one standing by the jukebox giggling like a crazy person.

"Oh, I hope so," my wife says with a happy sigh. "I really do."

"Me too." I smile and pull her into my arms for another kiss and another, knowing without a doubt that I'm the luckiest man on earth.

SNEAK PEEK FROM LILI VALENTE!

Check out this HOT new friends with bang-i-fits read from Lili Valente! THE BANGOVER is available now!

ABOUT THE BOOK

It started with too much whiskey, and ended with two plane tickets to Vegas and a make out session with my best friend, renegade rock star, Colin Donovan.

Kill me now...
No, seriously, kill me now. I'm begging you.

'Cause there's no way I'll make it through this Best Buddy Festival of Fornication with my dignity intact. The moment Colin and I do more than kiss, he's going to realize that my feelings for him run so much deeper than just friends.

I intend to fly back home as soon as our plane touches down —I can't risk losing Colin, not for all the Big O's in Sin City.

But then we run into his evil ex, inciting a series of events that includes chaos, dancing at midnight, more chaos, a cat in a purse, a mirror on a ceiling, multiple conspiracy theories, yet even more chaos, and Colin in my bed.

Yes. My bed.
And he's everything I've dreamed he would be, and more.

Maybe the high will be worth the fall.
All I know is that by the time we're done, we'll both have one hell of a Bangover.

Excerpt from THE BANGOVER

I wake up with no feeling in my right arm, my face smashed into an unfamiliar pillow, a case of cottonmouth any stuffed animal would be proud of, and the disturbing realization that I can't remember where I am or how I got here.

I can't remember, but I instantly know Colin is involved.

I am not a rock star.

I do not do rock-star things like stay up all night burning old love letters or go skinny-dipping in the ocean at midnight or drink so much whiskey after a show that building a pack of vampire snowmen in the town square at three a.m. sounds like a good idea. But under the influence of too much Colin Donovan, I have done all of these things and more.

And apparently, our latest case of shared insanity has landed me on a plane. There's no mistaking the lingering smell of jet fuel or the dull roar of the engines churning away on either side of this soaring death pellet.

I crack open my lids, and yes—there's the overhead bin,

dull gray and sad in the dim light of the darkened cabin. But instead of the usual packed sardine tin of people on either side of me, there's only a fully-reclined seat arranged head-to-toe with mine, a quaint swiveling bedside table, and gray plastic walls that grant this little cubby-for-two almost complete privacy.

There is, however, no sign of Colin.

But I wouldn't put it past him to talk me into buying a first-class ticket to somewhere and then drop me off at the airport before skipping off to do more exciting things. He knows I hate planes. I hate them so much that I usually have to be drunk, drugged, or both to force myself down the Jetway and into my assigned seat. But I've never booked a trip while under the influence. I make travel plans, arrange my life accordingly, and then I pop a Xanax like a civilized person twenty minutes before boarding.

This impulsive gallivanting is unacceptable. I don't usually do impulsive, not even in my work. I'm a plotter, not a seat-of-my-pants wordsmith. I know exactly how the vampire clowns became vampire clowns and who they're going to kill—and why—before I type a single word. And if I deviate from my outline, I feel anxious, unsettled, unmoored until I find my way back to the path and tie up any loose ends I've created.

I like the path.

I like knowing what's coming next.

I like waking up in my own bed with my own pillow and all my memories of the night before.

I like all of that...until I snap, decide I don't like it anymore, and do something fucking crazy. The last time I snapped, I moved to a yurt in Tibet for a month. The time before that I went cage-diving with sharks. And before that, I bought a bed and breakfast at a repo auction, without even seeing the inside. All of those things turned out okay in the end—I learned to meditate in Tibet, conquered my fear of sharks, and set my sister up as proprietor of a profitable business with only a few bumps along the way renovation-wise.

But I'm just waiting for the day when I do something impulsive that doesn't have a happy ending. And perhaps today is that day.

I have no idea what inspired me to drink such an inadvisable amount of whiskey. But as I reach for the water bottle on the table beside me, grateful my hangover doesn't appear to be too vicious, I vow never to do it again.

No more whiskey, no more pranks with Colin, no more...

"Pranks," I mutter as I twist off the cap and gulp down every drop of brain-restoring liquid. I remember hiding out under the back porch at my place for what seemed like forever, waiting for Shep to come outside so we could prank him. I remember Colin having an existential crisis about his inability to write songs, and then I remember...

I remember...

"Oh no. No, no." I sink farther down in my chair, tugging my blanket up to my chin to hide my flaming cheeks seconds before a shadow appears at the entrance to the swanky first-class cubby.

A shadow cast by the long, lanky, yet surprisingly well-muscled body of my best friend. A body I am well acquainted with seeing as I had my hands all over him last night. All over his chest, his biceps, his abs, his ass... The same lovely ass that moves across my field of vision as he climbs quietly over me to settle in his seat, clearly thinking I'm still asleep.

I squeeze my eyes shut and fight to keep my breath slow and even, but I'm a horrible actress, and Colin has superhero-like senses and reflexes. If he weren't a rock star, he could be a ninja assassin or a cat burglar or something more wholesome that involves a similar skill set, but which I can't think of at the moment because my mind is not naturally inclined to weave wholesome stories and because I am dying of shame.

Dying—my heart stuttering to a stop and my stomach turning to stone as Colin grabs a fistful of my blanket and tugs it down to reveal my face. "Hey there, sunshine," he says with a grin. "How you feeling this morning?"

I shake my head and tug the blanket back up.

"That good, huh?" He chuckles and pulls it back down. "Don't hide. Talk to me. How much do you remember?"

"Nothing," I lie, leaping at my one chance at salvation. "Nothing between going out to hide under the porch and waking up a few minutes ago. What happened? How did we get here?"

Colin's full lips purse, and his brown-and-amber-flecked eyes narrow. "Yeah? That's all?" He brushes a thoughtful thumb back and forth along the line of his jaw, the pad making a soft shushing sound as it disturbs his morning whiskers. He's rocking a seven-a.m. shadow that makes him look even more like a naughty rock star, but if memory serves, this time it isn't Colin who can't be trusted.

It's me.

The killer's call is coming from inside the house...

He leans closer. "So you don't remember kissing me last night?"

I shake my head, wide-eyed in what I hope looks like innocence mixed with utter shock.

"No? Really?" he murmurs, resting a hand on the curve of my hip, making my skin burn even through the covers and the long skirt I'm wearing beneath. "Then I guess you don't remember dragging me up to your room, stripping off all of your clothes, and riding me like the last roller coaster left standing?"

My eyeballs attempt to leap out of my skull, but thankfully there are muscles and ligaments in place to keep things like that from happening.

There are not, unfortunately, muscles in place to keep my tongue from flapping. "I did not, you dirty liar."

"So you do remember," he says, pointing a victorious finger at my face. "Now who's the dirty liar, Larry?"

SNEAK PEEK FROM PIPPA GRANT!

Love red-hot enemies to lovers, secrets, and marriage of convenience? Read on for a sneak peek at Pippa Grant's **Hot Heir**!

Viktor (aka a royal bodyguard who only thinks hot air is his biggest problem)

It'll be fine, Viktor, His Highness said.

Perfectly safe. Nothing to worry about, His Highness said.

You wouldn't want to disappoint Gracie, would you, Viktor? His Highness said.

In my twelve years as lead bodyguard to His Highness—Prince Manning Frey, third son of the king of Stölland—I've learned to never trust *It'll be fine, Viktor*.

But in the seven months since Miss Gracie Diamonte became a permanent fixture in His Highness's life, I've yet to learn that sometimes, she must be disappointed.

Were she unpleasant or loud-mouthed or the scheming sort—like the woman I currently find myself attempting to not throttle—it would be far easier to tell Miss Diamonte *no*. That it's not the best idea to take a balloon ride over town to view this *Grits Festival* from above. But His Highness has sworn his eternal love and allegiance to a woman sweeter than honey and kinder than a saint who also bakes the most marvelous cookies I've ever had the pleasure of tasting.

If angels are real, Miss Diamonte is surely one of them.

Again, very much unlike the woman I currently find myself struggling to not strangle.

Were we anywhere other than a hundred meters in the air in the scorching midday heat of a record-breaking Alabama summer day, held aloft only by the flame of a hot air balloon that neither of us knows how to operate, with sirens flashing on the roads below us as the local authorities attempt to chase us by ground, I would consider baiting this woman who is the very antithesis of His Highness's dear Miss Diamonte.

I do quite enjoy baiting Miss Peach Maloney when the opportunity presents itself.

At the moment, however, I'd far rather get us back safely to the ground. "Madame, you own a flight adventure company," I remind her. "I daresay this current predicament is *your* specialty."

So perhaps I'm not entirely capable of *not* baiting her. But I do stand by my statement that my priority is returning to the ground.

Especially seeing as *I* would not have dove into the hot air balloon basket to save Miss Maloney had *she* not been in the basket in the first place as it began to rise.

"I don't do the *flying*, and we operate *airplanes*, not *balloons*." Her blue eyes flash, and for the briefest of moments, I contemplate the likelihood of her being able to lever me out of this basket and send me careening to my death, as she, too, seems to be contemplating strangling me.

Reasonably unlikely that she might overpower me, I decide.

Which leaves room for error, as I don't deduct her chances to be nil.

I don't like it.

ABOUT THE AUTHORS

Pippa Grant is a USA Today Bestselling author who writes romantic comedies that will make tears run down your leg. When she's not reading, writing or sleeping, she's being crowned employee of the month as a stay-at-home mom and housewife trying to prepare her adorable demon spawn to be productive members of society, all the while fantasizing about long walks on the beach with hot chocolate chip cookies.

Find Pippa at...
www.pippagrant.com
pippa@pippagrant.com

Author of over forty novels, *USA Today* Bestseller Lili Valente writes everything from steamy suspense to laugh-out-loud romantic comedies. A die-hard romantic and optimist at heart, she can't resist a story where love wins big. Because love should always win.

When she's not writing, Lili enjoys adventuring with her two sons, climbing on rocks, swimming too far from shore, and asking "why" an incorrigible number of times per day. A former yoga teacher, actor, and dancer, she is also very bendy and good at pretending innocence when caught investigating off-limits places.

You can currently find Lili in the mid-South, valiantly trying to resist the lure of all the places left to explore.

Find Lili at www.lilivalente.com

ALSO BY THE AUTHORS

Sexy Motherpucker

Puck Aholic

Puck me Baby

Pucked up Love

Puck Buddies

The Red Hot Hunter Brothers

The Baby Maker

The Troublemaker

The Heartbreaker

The Panty Melter

Sexy Flirty Dirty Rom Coms

Magnificent D

Spectacular Rascal

Incredible You

Meant for You

The Bangover

Swoon-Worthy Cowboys

Leather and Lace

Saddles and Sin

Diamonds and Dust

Glitter and Grit

Chaps and Chance

Ropes and Revenge